BRANDED

It was hardly surprising that Latham Elliot should hate her brother Carl, Susi thought ruefully, after the terrible thing that Carl had done to him. But for the same reason it was hardly likely that Latham would think kindly of her, was it—let alone return her love for him?

BRANDED

BY

MARGARET MAYO

To Glad & Dave

With love

Margaret Mayo.

June 1984

MILLS & BOON LIMITED
15–16 BROOK'S MEWS
LONDON W1A 1DR

First published 1984
Australian copyright 1984

© Margaret Mayo 1984

ISBN 0 263 10562 8

Set in Monophoto Times 10 on 11 pt.
07–0684 – 55285

Made and printed in Great Britain by
Richard Clay (The Chaucer Press) Ltd,
Bungay, Suffolk

For Sheila
with love

CHAPTER ONE

SUSI's nerves jangled as she neared Kalabara. She could understand Carl moving if it meant travelling this distance every day—but he could have let them know! It was wrong of him to change his address without informing them. She had flown almost thirteen thousand miles expecting to find him, and the shock when she discovered he no longer lived there had been enormous. The present tenant of the flat was of no help, but fortunately one of his old neighbours remembered where he worked.

Susi kept her fingers mentally crossed that he had not left his job too without telling anyone where he was going. That would be the last straw.

Once they had left Sydney behind, the rolling Australian landscape stretched for mile upon mile with nothing to be seen but open plains and scrubland punctuated with isolated gum trees. In the far distance the parched brown turned to a haze of blue-green where the bush began, but before they reached this thick forest area they turned off the main road and followed a narrow dirt track which led eventually to a sprawling white house.

Grazing horses looked up uninterestedly as they passed. There was no other sign of life. Acres and acres of fields spread out on all sides. It was like the middle of nowhere.

'This *is* Latham Elliot's place?' she enquired carefully before settling with the taxi driver. Had she known how far Kalabara was she would have thought twice about hiring him, and maybe she ought to ask him to wait. Check that Carl was still here.

He nodded. 'Sure thing, lady. Is he expecting you?'

Susi shook her head, her wide unusual grey-green eyes faintly apprehensive. 'I've come to see my brother. He works here.'

The driver smiled, seeming satisfied, and before she could say another word set his car into motion. Soon he was nothing more than a cloud of dust. He had made up her mind for her.

She walked towards the white house, running an appraising eye over the building, liking what she saw. It was long and low with a series of arches which provided tempting glimpses into landscaped gardens beyond.

It was kept in immaculate order, and as she approached the front door, an old man with a khaki hat pulled low over a tanned leathery face appeared as if from nowhere.

'Aren't you a bit out of your way, miss? We don't have visitors here.'

The brusque words were daunting, but Susi eyed him hopefully.

'Are you Mr Elliot?'

The old man's straggly brows rose, his brow creasing into a thousand wrinkles. 'I'm his manager. Is he expecting you?'

Susi shook her head. 'But it's very important. I'd be obliged if you'd tell him I'm here.'

The man still looked doubtful. 'Mr Elliot sees no one—not without a prior appointment. Can you tell me what it's about?' He chewed on a piece of grass and looked as though he was prepared to stand there all day.

Susi began to feel irritated. What sort of a person was this Latham Elliot? 'It's about my brother,' she said, 'Carl Kingswood.'

The man's expression altered, a certain grimness coming to it. 'I'm sorry, miss, I'm even more sure now that Mr Elliot won't see you.'

She narrowed her eyes, feeling suddenly inexplicably apprehensive. 'I haven't come all this way to be fobbed off. I demand that you take me to him!'

He shrugged uneasily. 'If you insist, but——' He trailed off uncertainly. 'Please wait here, I'll see what I can do.'

He headed towards one of the arches, looking back anxiously over his shoulder before he disappeared. Susi was puzzled. He had neither confirmed nor denied that Carl still worked here. It was clear he knew of her brother—but there was something wrong. She wished she had questioned him further.

It seemed an age before the man returned. Susi had not moved from her spot, the strong Australian sun burning down on her head, making her wish she had had the good sense to wear a hat. It was one of those splendid days so rare in England, with not a cloud to be seen, no breeze to disturb the leaves of the gum trees or the feathery pines that grew close to the house.

It was how she had imagined Australia to be—hot and dry, with mile upon endless mile of barren plains. Unlike Sydney and its suburbs, which had disappointed her with its monumental traffic. She had no doubt that when she had time to explore the city she would feel differently. But her first impression had been disillusioning.

'Mr Elliot will see you,' said the old man, a look of surprise on his face, as though he had never expected him to agree. 'Follow me.'

She held her head that much higher as they entered the house, her heels clattering on the tiled floor, her eyes involuntarily taking in the opulence of her surroundings. Latham Elliot was a very rich man.

But she had no time to give it more than a cursory glance before she was shown into a room which was dominated by a huge desk set at right angles to the window, through which were superb views over the pastures which rolled away from the house.

The man at the desk made no attempt to stand as she entered. Indeed he did not even look at her. Susi immediately decided he was the rudest man she had ever met.

His legs were stretched out beneath the desk, his boot-clad feet protruding on the other side. A grey tee-shirt stretched tautly across a muscular chest, long arms looked strong and sinewy, covered with a thin layer of dark hair. He twirled a pencil between hard bony fingers, seeming more intent on that than on his unexpected visitor.

Black hair curled about a noble head. In profile his nose was straight and strong, his brow high and proud, jutting cheekbones giving an angular appearance to his face. His jaw was square and determined, thrust aggressively forward.

Eventually he glanced obliquely across. 'Miss Kingswood?'

Susi inclined her head, a pin falling from her hair as she did so, spilling some of its long auburn length about her face. She had purposely pinned it up so that the breeze would cool her nape, now she pushed it back with an impatient hand, returning Latham Elliot's gaze with as much dignity as she could muster.

He was not pleased to see her, that was for sure, suggesting there was no love lost between himself and her brother. But it was not Latham Elliot she had come to see. She could ignore his hostility for as long as it took her to find out where Carl was.

Forestalling her question, he said, 'If it's your brother you're after you can turn right round and go. Kingswood no longer works here.' The loathing in his voice, the condescending arrogance, was unmistakable, and the way he looked at her, as though he hated her as much as he did her brother, made her flinch.

She felt it much as she would a knife slicing through her flesh. It was with difficulty that she controlled a natural urge to back away. This man was vitriolic. 'Perhaps you could tell me where he is?'

Her heart hammered unsteadily, but she put it down to the shock of discovering Carl no longer worked here, rather than admit that this man's attitude had anything to do with it. Never had she felt so unwelcome. He really did loathe the very sight of her, which was puzzling, as they had only just met.

She forced herself to smile, wondering if playing the helpless female would get her anywhere—then doubted it. It was not really her scene anyway. She had always stood up for herself and she was sure that she was not going to let Latham Elliot intimidate her, even though it was what he was doing right at this moment. It was a peculiar feeling, one she had never experienced before. He had spoken no more than a few words, yet still she felt threatened.

'I have no idea.' The guttural denial also suggested that he was not interested.

'But you must know,' protested Susi. 'He's my brother, don't you understand that? I've come from England to see him.'

'I couldn't care less where you've come from,' he gritted coldly. 'You're not welcome. Please go.'

Susi shook her head and another pin came spinning free. With an angry gesture she pulled out all that remained, pushing back her hair with impatient fingers, hoping it did not look too much of a mess.

The room was air-conditioned and cool, but even so her palms were moist, her cotton blouse clinging damply to her back. 'Where do you suggest I go?' she demanded. 'I've come here by taxi—all the way from Sydney, in case you're interested. It's cost me a fortune. I thought I would find Carl here. Are you sure you don't know where he is?'

'If you're stupid enough to dismiss your taxi without ascertaining whether you're at the right place, then you're as idiotic as the rest of your sex. I suppose Jake will have to take you, and if you want my advice you'll catch the next plane back to England. There's nothing doing for you here.'

Susi tensed and strode over to the side of his desk, placing her hands on the edge, glaring into his eyes, which were as black and impenetrable as night, piercing her, probing her soul. She shuddered, his raw masculinity making itself felt for the first time.

In the course of her job she had met all sorts of men, but none so intimidating as this one. 'I refuse to go until you've told me where my brother is. You must know.'

Very slowly he pushed himself to his feet, and Susi wished she had kept her distance. Although she never thought of herself at five foot six as being small, this man towered almost a foot above her, a formidable strength emanating from him, coupled with a hostility that she found difficult to understand.

She discovered that although his shoulders were broad his hips were narrow, faded blue denims doing little to hide the powerful length of his legs.

'I am not in the habit of lying, Miss Kingswood. I do not know where your brother is, neither do I care. Is that clear?'

'Perfectly.' His voice had risen and Susi found difficulty in suppressing her anger. 'But I still think you might be able to help. You must have some idea. There's no one else I can ask.'

'And it's so important that you find him?' sneered Latham Elliot, his lips curled contemptuously.

'He hasn't written home in well over two years.' She fixed her wide eyes on his face, noting the harsh lines scored from nose to chin, creases about his eyes through continually squinting into the sun. He looked like a man who hated sitting behind a desk, who found it a necessary evil to be dealt with and disposed of as quickly as possible—and she had disturbed him!

'He never struck me as a mother's boy.'

'But he did write,' insisted Susi, 'when he first came out. We had a regular monthly letter. My parents were very upset when they stopped.'

A black scowl appeared, making him even more threatening, sending a nervous shiver down her spine. 'I don't see why you're telling me this. I have no interest in anything concerned with Carl Kingswood.'

'Okay, so you had some disagreement with him.' Susi's eyes were fiercely aggressive, 'but that's no reason why you shouldn't help me. I was planning on staying with Carl.'

'Then it's bad luck you're having,' fired Latham Elliot cruelly, sitting again, spinning his chair to stare out of the window.

Susi noted that his over-long hair, curling down the back of his neck, was as strong and wiry as the man himself. She had an insane urge to touch it. The cotton tee-shirt was stretched to the limit across his broad back, a wide leather belt sat low on his hips. Never had she seen a man who exuded such animal magnetism.

Compared with those she had met in England he was

rough and savage; barbaric, probably. There was an earthiness about him that was ironically appealing, exciting her, making her pulses leap. Nevertheless she felt an anger against him that was unusual for her. But then again, she had never come across anyone so openly hostile.

'I also came out on a one-way ticket,' claimed Susi loudly. 'It was all I could afford. If you won't help me, there's no way that I'll be able to find Carl.'

'That's your bad luck!' The harsh snarl was slung over his shoulder.

Susi's green eyes blazed brightly in her over-heated face. 'And that's all you care! Really, Mr Elliot, it wouldn't hurt you to help.'

'Are you suggesting that I'm lying?'

She wished he would turn. It was difficult speaking to a man's back. 'I'm suggesting that you're being deliberately awkward, that simply because you and he have had—words, you're taking it out on me.'

She heard his savage breath, but although she expected him to look at her he still stared through the window. At what, she had no idea. So far as she could see there was nothing for miles.

'You could try the police,' he suggested indifferently. 'Report him as a missing person.'

'And what good would that do?' she demanded. 'They'd be sure to come here and ask you, and if you're as difficult with them as you are with me they'd have nothing to go on.'

His shoulders lifted in an indifferent shrug. 'That's your hard luck.'

'What I want to know,' she said crossly, 'is what happened to the letters we sent him. Surely they were forwarded. Did he live here after moving from his flat?'

Slowly Latham Elliot half turned and again she saw

his face in profile. Never had she seen a man so proud, so arrogant, so full of aggression, as though he had a grudge against the whole world.

'He has never lived here. I don't know what's happened to your letters. Perhaps it was the same time as——' He stopped, and although it was difficult to see his face clearly with the sunlight blazing behind him, she did not miss the tightening of those cruelly curved lips, the hardening of the jet eyes. '—as he left my employ.'

'Why did he leave?' Susi thought it a perfectly reasonable question, was unprepared when he rammed a fist into the palm of his hand.

'Because he valued his life!'

There was such venom in his tone that Susi's head jerked sharply, her eyes widening, her thick lashes framing them dramatically. 'You threatened him?'

'I have no wish to discuss Carl Kingswood,' he said stiffly. 'Please go! I have nothing more to say to you.'

But Susi had no intention of being put off. 'You're clearly withholding some information that could be of use to me. Why?'

A sneer curled his lips. 'Would it surprise you if I said that it was because I didn't want to disillusion you?' Thick brows rose, cutting black eyes piercing her face.

Susi shrugged. 'Okay, so my brother isn't a saint. I wouldn't know about that. I haven't seen him since I was fourteen, and he's ten years older than me. I never really had much to do with him.'

'Then why chase after him now?'

'Because he's all the family I have left. My parents died a few months ago. As a matter of fact, they were going to come out here as soon as my father retired, but unfortunately they were involved in a rather nasty road accident.' She was unable to keep a break from her voice. Not that she expected any compassion from this man, nor did she get it.

His voice was as hard and hostile as ever. 'So you thought you'd join forces with your dear brother? Take my advice, Miss Kingswood, and clear right out. No one with your name is welcome.'

Susi stiffened, wondering how she was going to get through to this despicable man. 'Whatever my brother has done I see no reason why you should take it out on me. If you'd just co-operate, at least give me some idea where you think he might have gone, then I'll go too. I don't like being here any more than you like having me.'

'For the last time,' said Latham Elliot impatiently, 'I have no idea where your brother is, nor do I wish to know. *If I did I'd kill him!*'

There was such venom in his tone that Susi involuntarily gasped, and stepped back a pace.

He eyed her coldly. 'You look surprised. Have you never seen a man with his heart full of hatred?'

Susi shook her head. 'I can't imagine that he could have done something so wrong that you still condemn him after—how long? Two years? You're a hard man, Mr Elliot. I imagine my brother was as anxious to leave your employ as you were to get rid of him.'

'Oh, he was anxious all right.' The bitter tones were loud, vibrating round the room, shaking the shelves. 'When someone is shooting at you, you certainly don't stand around long enough to argue.'

Susi was appalled. 'Are you saying that he was turned off your premises at gun-point?'

His broad shoulders lifted in an indifferent shrug. 'I am, and you're as unwelcome as he was. I want nothing to do with any of the Kingswood family. They leave a nasty taste in my mouth.'

Such was the venom in his tone that Susi felt a chill steal over her. Whereas before she had been perspiring, now she felt clammy and cold. Her heart raced and there was an unusual weakness in her legs. He should be reported to the police. Surely no person had the right to turn a gun on a fellow man? He was dangerous! He was insane! Her eyes were brightly green as she glared at him. 'Welcome or not, Mr Elliot,' she said loudly, 'you've made me even more determined to stay. I intend getting to the bottom of this business. You're crazy! You can't do things like that to people—it's against the law.' Her chest heaved as she fought for control.

'When you're afraid for your own life you don't think about what's right and what's wrong.'

Susi frowned. 'Carl was threatening *you*?' She could not believe that her brother would do such a thing.

With a sudden savage movement Latham Elliot sprang towards her and for the first time she saw him full face. 'He did more than threaten me,' he growled. 'He did this!'

He jutted his jaw, and Susi recoiled in horror when she saw the unsightly scar streaking his cheek.

'Carl—did that?' Her words were a strangled cry from the back of her throat.

'Repulses you, does it?' His lips curled and with a sudden unexpectedness he snatched her hand, pulling it against his face, making her feel the ragged line that gouged his jaw. 'How would you like to live with this?' he demanded savagely. 'Bear this mark for the rest of your life? This is what your brother did. Is it any wonder that I hate him?'

Her face paled and she tried to pull away.

He laughed, a deep unpleasant sound. 'It makes you feel sick? How do you think I feel? What do you think it's done to my life?'

Susi shook her head, nausea rising in her throat. She was unable to swallow, could only turn away from the tell-tale scar beneath her trembling fingers, her eyes wide and enormous in her pale face.

'I didn't know,' she managed to husk at last.

'The hell you didn't,' he cried. 'And now you can't bear to look at me. No woman likes to see a man disfigured. No woman could stand me touching her. Is that right?'

With an abruptness that startled her he let go her hand and caught her face instead between his hard fingers. He compelled her to look at him, and although she rigorously kept her eyes off the scar the piercing quality of his eyes was equally disconcerting.

She knew he was going to kiss her even before his mouth possessed hers, and it was impossible to quell a feeling of panic. She ought never to have come here. He was insane!

She closed her eyes, but even though she could no longer see the blazing eyes, the ugly blemish, she could not forget, and she struggled feverishly, trying to ignore the fact that this man's kiss was affecting her in an entirely unexpected way.

There was an expertise behind it which suggested there had been many women in his life, although she would hazard a guess that he had treated none of them as brutally as he was doing her now. Her lips were ground back against her teeth until she tasted the salt of blood, his bony fingers bruising the soft skin of her face. Yet despite all this there was a thread of awareness running through her. Despite his anger, despite his aggression, she found him amazingly, a sexually attractive man.

It was insanity, there was no rhyme nor reason behind it, yet it was a fact. She was responding to him as she had never responded to anyone in her life. The discovery made her struggle all the harder, and when at length he put her from him there was derision in his eyes.

'Now you see why I don't want you here. You've brought it all back, the whole damn mess. As if I need reminding that I'm offensive! As if I haven't suffered enough!'

'My God, you feel sorry for yourself!' cried Susi. 'How was I supposed to know? Tell me that, will you?'

He shook his head, his eyes blazing maniacally. 'Get out!'

'Not until you tell me what happened. I think at least you owe me that.'

Their eyes met and held for a few long seconds and such was his power that Susi could not look away even though she wanted to.

At length he turned and sat down heavily at the desk. 'Your not so perfect brother helped himself to my profits. He *kindly* offered to lend a hand with the books when they became too much for me, and in so doing lined his own pockets. Naturally when I accused him he denied it, but when I said I was going to call in an independent auditor to check my accounts he turned nasty.' Again his lip curled contemptuously.

'We were out riding at the time, exercising two of my best stallions. When our conversation turned into a full-scale argument I dismounted and suggested he do the same. I said that if he owned up to cooking my books and paid back all that he'd taken nothing more would be said.

'But that didn't suit your brother. He lost his temper completely and turned the horse on me. Black Knight had always been wild, and with Carl shouting and whipping, hauling on the reins, charging him at me, he needed no encouragement. I stood no chance.' There was pain in his eyes as he relived those moments.

'If you've ever had your ribs crushed by a horse's hooves, or your face smashed in, you'd know why I feel so bitter. I was certain he would stamp me to death and there was nothing at all I could do about it.'

Susi clapped her hand to her mouth as she listened to his portrayal. How could Carl have done this? What on earth had possessed him?

'Fortunately Jake came riding by. He took out his gun and shot the horse. I wish to God he'd shot Carl instead.'

Susi felt physically sick. 'And then what?' She did not want to believe him, but no man would have made up such a story. The scar on his face was living proof.

'We didn't see Carl's backside for dust. By the time Jake had reassured himself I was not dead Carl was gone. With one of my most valuable horses killed, not to mention the hundreds of dollars he had milked me of, you can see why even his name is anathema, and why I don't want you here. So get the hell out. *Now!*'

He dropped his head in his hands, his shoulders hunched. Susi knew there was nothing she could say, no words to ease the hatred in his heart, no atonement for the wrong her brother had done.

Thank goodness, she thought, that her parents had never found out. They had been so proud of him. They thought he was doing so well for himself. Slowly she turned and walked towards the door, wondering what she was going to do next.

She would have to find a job, she supposed, save up until she had enough money to resume her search for Carl—or go back to England. Her parents had not been well off and there had been little left after paying for the funeral. It had been a shock to discover that neither of them had been insured, and as the house was rented, there was no money from that either.

She gave up the tenancy when coming out here, thinking she might settle down with her brother. She had never expected to find anything like this.

She was outside the door when his harsh demanding voice halted her. 'Miss Kingswood!'

She turned and looked enquiringly into his narrow-eyed stare, feeling a shiver of apprehension, convinced that whatever he was going to say would not be pleasant.

'I've decided that *you* shall repay me. You will stay here and work until such time as I consider your brother's debt paid.'

Susi was stunned. 'You mean work for *you*—for *nothing*?' The man was mad! He was a raving lunatic! The accident had affected his brain.

He inclined his head. 'It's the least you can do. I happen to need a cook and housekeeper right now. It will save me the trouble of advertising.'

'Cook?' Susi was even more incredulous. 'Mr Elliot, I'm not a domestic!'

'All women can cook,' he said positively. 'And by your own admittance you need a roof over your head, so it will solve both our problems.'

'Are you forgetting that my presence here will continue to remind you of my brother?'

The scorn in her voice was not lost on him, but he said gravely, 'I'm not forgetting, but I hope my pleasure in seeing you suffer will outweigh the disadvantages.'

'I refuse to listen to any more of your insanities!' declared Susi, swinging round and heading for the door.

But he was behind her instantly, gripping her wrist, yanking her back into the room.

'You're mad!' she accused. 'You can't do this to
me—I won't let you!'

'You have no choice,' he ground. 'You certainly
won't get far if you try to run away. As you must have
noticed, we're pretty isolated.'

She glared hostilely, her eyes flashing with an anger
that she had rarely experienced before meeting this
man. 'But you intend keeping me here? What kind of a
man are you, Mr Elliot? Perhaps my brother wasn't far
wrong when he attacked you. How do I know you
didn't accuse him wrongly? You're not being very fair
on me.'

'Nor will I be,' he snarled. 'I hoped that one day I'd
meet up with Carl Kingswood, but you'll do just as
well.'

Susi trembled beneath the ferociousness of his words,
but stared back bravely. 'You don't frighten me, Mr
Elliot. There's no way you can hold me here against my
will. I'll phone the police. Tell me, are all Australians as
uncivilised as you?'

He glared. 'If you find my methods unorthodox then
you have only your brother to blame. I have always
prided myself on being fair.'

'But because you've got a scar on your face you're
now taking it out on everyone else. Is that it?' jeered
Susi, tilting her chin and looking up rebelliously into
the blackness of his eyes.

His lips curved in a smile that held no humour. 'Quite
a spitfire, aren't you? That's good. You'll need spirit
because, believe me, I intend making you suffer just as
much as your brother did me.'

'You swine! You can't do this to me, I won't let you!'
She again made for the door, wrenching it open, shooting
Latham Elliot a furious glare. But her exit was barred by
the old man and she came to a sudden full stop.

'Ah, Jake!' Latham seemed to know he would be there. 'Miss Kingswood has kindly agreed to stay on as housekeeper. Perhaps you'd show her to her room?'

Jake looked surprised but accepted the situation without question, giving Susi a gap-toothed grin. 'You're very welcome. The hands will be glad of a good feed. I've received nothing but complaints ever since I took over the cooking!'

Susi glanced coldly at Latham Elliot before saying, 'If I were you I wouldn't be so jubilant. I'm not such a good cook either.'

'You can't be worse'n me,' admitted Jake good-naturedly, and led the way through a series of arches until they came to a room at the far end of one of the corridors. 'This will be yours. I'm afraid it's been left as it was since Mrs Riley left. None of us has time for cleaning rooms.'

'I take it Mr Elliot isn't married?' asked Susi, staring in dismay at the unmade bed. The whole room looked as though a tornado had whistled through it.

When she got no answer she turned, only to discover that Jake had gone. Angrily she slammed the door, surveying the disorder, her rage increasing by the minute. Just who did Latham Elliot think he was? He could not do this to her. She would not let him!

Savagely she yanked open the door. She would tell him exactly what she thought of him—and his job. She stopped short when she was confronted by the man himself, her suitcases held in either hand.

'Mr Elliot——' she began, but he brushed her aside and deposited her cases in the room.

'There will only be Jake and myself for dinner this evening.' His tones were crisp. 'But there'll be eight for breakfast. The men arrive early and expect a good meal after they've done a couple of hours' work.

They also have their lunch here, but naturally go home at night.'

'Naturally,' repeated Susi, not bothering to hide her sarcasm. 'But I'm not staying. I refuse to be browbeaten by you!'

'The way I see it you have no choice.' His tone was calm, but it did not deceive her. 'There's nowhere you can go.'

She glared. 'Not at the moment, maybe, but when I've gathered my wits, when I've got over my jet-lag, have no fear, Mr Elliot, I shall get away from here.'

'Don't try it,' he rapped, 'because believe me, you'll wish you never had!' He disappeared before she could respond and when he had gone she sat down on the edge of the bed fuming, more angry than she had ever been in her life. She was also very, very tired. She was quite sure she would not have enough energy to make her bed and put away her clothes, let alone cook a meal for Latham Elliot and Jake.

But Susi was a fighter if nothing else, and if this man thought he was going to bring her to her knees he was mistaken. Maybe cooking and housekeeping weren't in her line but she had no doubt she could cope—if she had to. And at the moment there seemed to be no option.

With a sudden burst of energy she opened her cases and hung away her clothes, finding fresh sheets for the bed in the linen press next to her room. After that she took a shower and changed into a cotton dress, brushing back her hair and tying it in her nape with a length of ribbon.

She found the kitchen without too much problem. It was big and had every modern convenience, although at this moment it was as untidy as any kitchen she had seen. Jake clearly did no more than was absolutely necessary. Dirty dishes were piled in the sink, the remains of lunch still sat on the stove.

Susi discovered a big overall behind the door and began the job of getting the room into order. It did not take long. She was a quick worker and soon it was spotless.

There was steak in the fridge and potatoes in a rack outside the kitchen door. Steak and chips should go down well, she thought, even though she was not hungry herself.

Never had she eaten so much in her life as she had on the plane. Every four hours a meal was placed in front of them, and by the end of the twenty-five-hour flight she had felt like a balloon. Food was the last thing she wanted at this moment.

As soon as dinner was cooked the two men appeared as if by magic. Jake smiled, his lined face creasing into a thousand wrinkles, and gleefully rubbed his hands. Latham Elliot, on the other hand, showed no emotion, eating solidly, both of them disappearing as soon as they had finished.

Susi felt choked. They could at least have thanked her! When the kitchen was once again tidy she went to her room, and as soon as her head touched the pillow was asleep.

She was awoken by someone pounding on her door. For a moment she could not think where she was. The white walls, the flower-sprigged bedspread, the pine furniture, they were all unfamiliar.

'Do I have to come in and wake you?' Latham Elliot's voice brought memories flooding back.

Susi groaned, recalling all too vividly that she was supposed to cook breakfast for his employees. She was still so tired! But she was certainly not going to give him the pleasure of seeing her fall down on the job he had imposed upon her. She had her pride.

'I'm coming!' she called briskly, glancing at her watch, surprised to see it was after eight. She sprang out of bed and crossed to the window. Wire mesh prevented mosquitoes entering, but it hid none of the beauty of the garden.

There were palms and pines and flowers of every hue imaginable. A sprinkler kept the lawns green and lush—and she could see the edge of a swimming pool! Such luxury! She promised herself a dip later, meantime hurrying to get dressed and begin her day's work.

It amazed her how she had accepted the situation. She ought to have put up a stronger fight. There was no way that Latham Elliot could do this to her. Yet she was letting him! Was agreeing to become his—slave!

Unless it was that kiss? It had certainly affected her. She recalled it now for the first time, and her cheeks burned. It had been savage and punishing, brutal in the extreme, a kiss that had shattered her to the core, leaving her in no doubt that Latham Elliot was a sexually aggressive man.

He had the ability to arouse a woman, yet because of what her brother had done had condemned himself to celibacy. He had become hard and bitter and was now taking a barbaric delight in pouring all the hatred he felt for Carl on her.

She would need all her strength. But this morning the challenge did not daunt her. Although still not completely refreshed, she felt much better than she had last night, and sticking up to Latham Elliot would be a battle she would enjoy.

She showered in the green adjoining bathroom. It was expensively furnished, as seemed to be everything about this place, but because she was already late Susi spent no time admiring her surroundings.

Once she had towelled herself dry she wriggled into a

pair of tight jeans, adding a blouse that tied in a knot at her waist, scraping back her thick auburn hair into a ponytail.

The kitchen was empty, for which she was thankful. She had had a mental picture of Latham Elliot waiting with darkened brow, demanding to know what had taken her so long.

Bearing in mind the fact that she had eight men to feed, Susi cooked a couple of dozen rashers of bacon, plenty of thick succulent sausages, two eggs each, plus a saucepan of baked beans and a pile of fried bread. She had no idea what the men usually had for breakfast, but decided they could not go wrong with good old English bacon and egg.

At the far end of the kitchen was an oblong table with a bench at either side. She set it out with knives and forks and no sooner was the food ready than the men appeared. They were a rough lot, eyeing her trim figure with appreciation, especially her bare midriff and the deep vee at the neck of her blouse.

But even more than admiring her figure did they enthuse over the food. Latham was the last to make his appearance, his jet eyes flicking over her coldly as he took his seat at the head of the table. His curt, 'Thanks,' when she placed his meal before him was the only word that he spoke.

Susi eyed him discreetly from her end of the kitchen. He wore a black tee-shirt this morning, making him look even more menacing than before. There was a lethal quality about him. He reminded her of a black panther. He had that loose-limbed grace that all jungle animals have. She decided his eyes should have been green rather than black, they would have completed the picture perfectly.

There was an air of withdrawal about him and she

noticed that the men did not include him in their conversation. She wondered whether it was the accident that had made him retreat into himself, whether before he had been at one with his employees. It had certainly scarred his mind as well as his face. She guessed it would be with him for all time.

After the men had finished eating and drunk gallons of tea—she had brewed it thick and strong which they seemed to appreciate—they filed out of the kitchen, only Latham Elliot remaining.

He lit up a thin cheroot and exhaled the smoke, eyeing her narrowly through the blue haze. 'That was definitely an improvement on Jake's cooking.'

She eyed him warily as she stacked the dirty plates. 'Is that supposed to be a compliment?'

'It's not my habit to hand out compliments,' he said tersely. 'Any woman could do better than Jake.'

'I should have known,' she muttered beneath her breath, but he heard and his face hardened.

'A word of warning, Miss Kingswood. Most of my men are married and I want no trouble in that quarter. I saw the way some of them were looking at you.'

'The way any man looks at a woman,' exploded Susi, 'unless he's made out of stone. It's your own life you're ruining, shutting everyone out the way you do. But if you think you're going to take your spite out on me, you're mistaken. I'm pretty tough when it comes to dealing with men—I've had to be.'

'You've come across some pretty unsavoury characters, then?' He looked as though the idea pleased him.

Susi shot him a scornful glance. 'That's what you'd like to think, I have no doubt. But you're wrong, Mr Elliot, I'm talking about work. I'm an electronics engineer—and let me tell you it was one hell of a job getting myself accepted!'

His eyes slid over her body, starting at her ankles, working their way up her denim-clad legs, over the smooth flatness of her stomach, lingering on the exposed flesh at her waist, pausing even longer where the striped cotton of her blouse outlined the pert thrust of her breasts.

By the time he reached her face Susi's pulses were labouring and it was all she could do to control her breathing. He had made no attempt to disguise the raw hunger he felt, and she wondered how long he had been without a woman.

He looked like a virile man who needed his physical desires satisfying pretty frequently. Not that she had any pity for him. It was his own fault if he felt his scar made him unattractive. Admittedly it was not pretty, but it was certainly not as off-putting as he seemed to think. One could get used to it—in time.

At the moment her eyes were drawn to it each time she looked at him, more so because it was her own brother who had done this to him. But she could imagine that any woman who loved him would not even notice it. It could in fact be to his advantage. It made him look as though he lived dangerously!

And she was being fanciful!

'Electronics, eh? You amaze me.'

'Do I?' asked Susi caustically. 'As a matter of fact I don't see that it's any concern of yours what I do. And it's certainly nothing at all to do with you the way your men look at me. I shan't be here long enough for any of them to try anything on.'

The lines of his face tightened, his cheekbones jutting through the flesh. He was too thin, she thought, but his rugged gaunt air was attractive nevertheless. Despite her antagonism Susi found herself drawn towards him and again recalled the feel

of his lips against hers, her whole body responding
unexpectedly.

'You'll be here for as long as I want you,' he said
thickly, threateningly. 'Don't ever forget that, not for
one minute. I have no intention of letting you go.'

Susi wondered how she could possibly feel magnetised
by so hard a man, and pushing all thoughts of his kiss
from her began furiously to stack the plates again. 'I'm
a free agent, Mr Elliot. When I'm ready to go I shall,
and you'll be unable to stop me.'

He smiled bitterly. 'You'll get no help from anyone
here, I've made sure of that. And it's a mighty long
walk to the nearest town. I hardly think that a slip of a
girl like you will be able to make it.'

Stiffening defensively, Susi said, 'You think we're all
weak and helpless, is that it? Let me tell you, Mr Elliot,
that when I make up my mind to do something I do it!'

His smile widened, revealing even white teeth, made
to look even whiter by the depth of his tan. Susi wished
nastily that the horse had smashed those too. 'Miss
Kingswood, I too do not change my mind once it's
made up.'

'Then it will be a battle of wills,' she snapped. 'I
might be a woman, but I'm definitely not inferior. I
believe in equality. Anything you care to hand out I can
take. Believe me, I'm not going to be the loser.'

'Interesting!' he drawled, pushing himself up. 'I must
admit you're taking this better than I expected.'

Susi allowed herself to smile. 'Never judge a book by
its cover, Mr Elliot. Now, if you wouldn't mind getting
out of the kitchen, I'd like to carry on with my work.'

She was finding it difficult to breathe. Latham
Elliot's presence was claustrophobic, to say the least.
Never had she met a man so aggressively masculine.
She wondered how she could possibly hate him yet feel

attracted at the same time. It was a situation she had never been in before. It was confusing and did not help her decision to leave. One half of her wanted to go, the other wanted to stay and find out exactly what made this embittered man tick.

CHAPTER TWO

AFTER two days at Kalabara Susi began to get into the routine. Although it left her with little time to herself she found the work more enjoyable than she had expected. It was an impressive house, built on clean, pleasing lines, each of the six bedrooms having its own *en suite* bathroom. But as only her own and Latham's were in use it took no more than a few minutes to clean them out each day.

Jake had his own flat built beneath the main part of the house, and he looked after this himself.

Susi did not see very much of Latham Elliot, apart from mealtimes when he kept a strict eye on her behaviour, fearing, no doubt, that she would fraternise with the men.

After their evening meal he usually disappeared into his study and she knew that it was often well into the early hours before he went to bed. He was up again at five, and she wondered how long he had maintained this rigorous pace.

She had a feeling it might have been since the affair with her brother and amazingly felt a shade guilty, not that she should have done. Latham Elliot was taking the whole thing too seriously.

On the third day Susi decided to take that promised dip in the pool. The work was done and she had an hour to spare before preparing their evening meal. The weather was unchanged, something that she had great difficulty in getting used to after the unpredictability of the English weather.

She put on a scarlet bikini which showed off to perfection her long slender limbs and the proud thrust of her breasts. She had no fear that she might bump into any of the men because they all worked well away from the house. Nevertheless she draped a towel about her shoulders just in case she bumped into anyone, Latham's warning echoing in her ears.

She made her way across the paved patio to the pool, which was shielded on three sides with a decorative screen wall, over which grew a splendid purple bougainvillaea. There were tables and chairs, and cushioned loungers, and as she slid into the inviting silken water Susi decided it was paradise. A little bit of heaven set into this baking Australian countryside.

After swimming until she was exhausted Susi relaxed on one of the brightly patterned sun-beds. In no time at all she was dry. Aware that the sun was stronger than that in England, she smoothed oil into her skin and lay down again on her stomach, closing her eyes, thinking that this wasn't a bad life after all.

Latham had kept her here to pay a debt, but if this was a penal sentence then no way was it severe. She was getting her meals and somewhere to sleep entirely for nothing.

Naturally there would come a time when she would need to earn some money, when the small amount she had brought with her was used up, but meanwhile she could think of nothing more pleasant than spending her time here at Kalabara, especially when the hateful Latham Elliot kept out of her way.

She decided that as she had not seen much of him he must be satisfied with what she was doing. Certainly there had been no complaints from any of the men. They ate with relish the meals she put before them, and judging by the goodnatured bantering between them they were happy in their work.

Latham Elliot might be a strict boss, but he must treat them fairly, because they certainly respected him. None of them would surely have remained had he been unreasonable?

Susi was startled out of her reverie when Latham's deep-throated voice exploded into the silence. 'I don't recall giving you permission to use the pool. You're supposed to be working!'

Rolling over on to her back, she shaded her eyes from the sun. Seen from this angle he looked taller than before, his denim-clad legs reaching ever upwards, his hard-muscled chest heaving beneath the thin cotton vest. He was one hell of an aggressive male, sensuous in the extreme—but that did not mean she was losing her head over him!

'I've finished all that needs doing.' With difficulty she held on to her temper. Latham Elliot rubbed her up the wrong way without even trying. Whenever they met she was instantly on the defensive, and at this moment, when he was accusing her of taking off time from work that she had already done, she was more incensed than ever.

'I'm quite sure,' he said strongly, 'that there's something else you can do. Mrs Riley never stopped. Do you mean to tell me you're more capable than she?'

Susi pushed herself up to a sitting position, glaring aggressively. 'It would appear so. If you care to inspect the house I'm quite sure you'll find nothing that needs doing.' How dared he speak to her like that!

The piercing eyes were unnerving, nevertheless she did not give him the satisfaction of looking away. 'Indeed I may just do that,' he said coldly. 'Even so, it doesn't give you a right to use this pool without permission.'

Susi lifted her chin and glared belligerently. 'You're

really quite the most obnoxious man I've ever met! What's wrong with you? Don't you like sharing your possessions? What harm am I doing? I've not seen anyone else use it, not even you. It's a crying shame to neglect it.'

'If I had the time,' he snarled savagely, 'I'd be in there most of the day. As you must have noticed, we do have work to do around here. It leaves little time for idling away the hours in the pool.'

'Then you should organise yourself better,' said Susi primly. 'It's taken me two days, no more, to get into a routine and, with your permission, of course,' her sarcasm was thinly veiled, 'I intend using this pool each afternoon. Why don't you join me?' Why she had thrown in this offer she had no idea, and she regretted it instantly.

Latham Elliot's eyes narrowed until there was nothing to be seen except two black slashes where his lashes bit together, his lips thinning impatiently. 'In my book a woman never issues the invitation. You're surely not trying to get round me?'

'As if I'd dare!' cried Susi.

'Then you'd do me a favour if you'd remove yourself from my presence. I had a notion to use the pool—but it will be by myself.'

Susi had no intention of being hustled away from the first relaxation she had enjoyed. 'Don't worry,' she said smoothly, 'I won't disturb you. I'm quite content to lie here and soak up the sun.'

'Or get sunburnt,' he said scathingly. 'Your back's as red as a beetroot. You're going to be hellishly sore tomorrow.'

'Then I'll toast my front.' Susi calmly lay down again, closing her eyes, assuming a nonchalance she was far from feeling. Who did he think he was trying to shove around? If he thought he was going to get the better of her he had chosen the wrong person. She had learned the hard way that working in a man's world meant being tough and determined, letting no one put on her.

There was silence, and when she next opened her eyes he had gone. She smiled. A minor triumph! She guessed it was the first time a woman had got the better of Latham Elliot. It made her feel good, at least ten feet tall.

Again she relaxed, listening to the birds squabbling in the tree-tops. There were all sorts of different sounds—warbles and cackles, shrieks, piercing whistles. She wondered how long it would be before she was able to distinguish the different birds.

There were magpies galore feeding on the lawns that surrounded Kalabara, much bigger than the ones in England. Blackbirds too, whose cry was strangely like the bleat of a lamb, and tiny blue wrens with their tails flicked up. But there were also brightly coloured birds that were unfamiliar. Had Latham joined her she could have asked him to identify them.

For a further ten minutes Susi lay there before deciding that she had had enough. Indoors it was beautiful and cool after the heat of the sun, and she took a long cold shower, dismayed to see that Latham had been right and her back was indeed as red as a turkeycock. She smoothed on an after-sun cream, but it was still burning strongly when she went through to the kitchen to begin preparations for their meal.

She had grown quite friendly with Jake, finding him more easy to get on with than the aggressive owner of the house, and the old man had taken a liking to her too. He admitted being surprised that Latham had

given her the job of housekeeper, but was dismayed
when she told him he was not paying her.

'He said it was my duty,' she declared. 'I was the
closest he would get to my brother, so I could pay off
his debts.'

'Typical!' snorted Jake angrily. 'He's been a difficult
man since the accident, but I don't agree with that. Let
me know if it gets too much, I'll have a word with him.'

Susi shook her head, smiling confidently. 'It's a
pleasure rather than a chore. This is a beautiful house. I
really love it here. But don't tell Latham or he might
send me away.'

Over their meal Jake and Latham discussed the new
stable block he was planning to build. The old man's
views differed from Latham's, and Susi was surprised
when he gravely considered Jake's point of view. Her
impression had been that he was a man who had his
own decided opinions and nothing or no one would
change them.

It grew dark surprisingly early, dusk lasting for no
more than half an hour, but even so the air was warm, and
after she had washed up Susi took a walk in the gardens.

They were lovely. Regular watering kept them green
and flourishing. There were bird of paradise flowers,
their blue and gold heads looking exactly like a bird.
There were geraniums bigger than any she had ever seen
in England, roses too; all the old familiar flowers, plus
lots of new ones. Plants that bloomed at different
seasons back home all flowering together here. An
incredible wonderland.

When she heard a splash in the pool she headed in its
direction without giving a second thought to who might
be using it. The bulbous lamps set at intervals about the
area illuminated it perfectly, and she was just in time to
see Latham hauling himself out.

The hard-muscled strength of his body took her breath away. There was not an ounce of superfluous flesh anywhere. He was vibrantly masculine, his black trunks fitting his lean hips snugly, his legs firm and muscled, dark wet hairs clinging to his chest. She could not take her eyes off him.

Not realising he was being observed, Latham shook his head like a dog, the flying droplets of water sparkling in the lamplight. It was several seconds before he saw Susi standing there.

'Get away!' The harshness of his voice made her jump. It had been remarkably peaceful, now his strident tones jarred the air.

'Why?' She thought it a logical question.

'Because I damn well don't want you here. Isn't that reason enough?'

Susi shrugged and took a step or two closer towards him. 'It's such a beautiful night, I don't blame you taking a swim. You work too hard.'

'And is that any business of yours?' he snarled.

'I suppose not.' She advanced more slowly, not daring to argue. It was not until she was a few feet away that she discovered the reason he had not wanted her to see him in the pool.

His chest was so badly scarred it was unbelievable. Yet another example of the torture he had received at the hands of her brother!

She closed her eyes, shaking her head in horror and dismay. 'I didn't know. I'm so sorry.' A lump rose in her throat and she had difficulty in swallowing.

'Sorry be damned!' he slammed at her. 'Perhaps it's as well you have seen. Now you know the type of man your brother really was.' With fingers of steel he gripped her shoulders, shaking her angrily, forcing her to look at the disfiguring marks just as he had compelled her to touch the scar on his face.

'I can't understand him,' she said quietly. 'I really can't. I wish there was something I could say, but there isn't. It's awful!'

'You're too right it is—it's bloody awful! I was a flaming mug for ever having taken Carl on. He had a violent temper, although I must admit it wasn't often he used it—usually when he was drunk. Do you have a temper, Miss Kingswood?'

Susi tore her eyes away from the damning evidence, looking into his face, appalled to see the brutality stamped there. 'I never thought I had—until—I came here,' she answered honestly. 'No one has ever spoken to me the way you do. But if it's any consolation I can see why you're so against me. I think I ought to leave. This can't be easy for you.'

'For God's sake shut up!' he spat viciously. 'If you think playing on my sympathy will make me get rid of you you're mistaken. It's a novelty now, looking after this house. I can see that you're enjoying it, but believe me, it won't last. It will become a chore, and that's when your debt will begin to be paid. You'll want to get out and meet people instead of having to put up with no one but me.'

'You're forgetting,' said Susi distantly, 'that there's Jake—and the rest of the men. I'm not lacking for company.'

'You're out of bounds so far as everyone except Jake is concerned.' His tones were bitterly aggressive, the lines of his face taut and angry. 'And Jake's too old to be a threat.'

'You're not thinking by any chance that I might crave male company? That I might become frustrated?' suggested Susi icily. 'If that's in your mind, forget it.'

His brows rose jeeringly. 'Are you implying that you

have no interest in sex? That you're one of those career women who put their work in front of everything else? You don't look the type to be a spinster.'

'I was not aware that there was any particular type,' she returned primly. 'I'm quite sure there's no woman who remains unmarried by choice. I have no doubt that one day I will get married and raise a family, but that time has not yet come. There's no man I've met who I've felt I couldn't live without. Most men are after only one thing, and so far as I'm concerned that's simply not on.'

'A virtuous female?' he sneered. 'I simply don't believe it.' He looked at her long and hard before shooting out a firm hand to curve round her waist, the other hooking itself beneath her heavy fall of hair, forcing her up against the sinuous hardness of his body.

There was no escape. His lips claimed hers brutally, deliberately, and although her mind was outraged it was impossible to stop her senses spinning.

As he explored the softness of her mouth his hands began a slow exploration of her body, sliding from her throat to her shoulders, moving with tantalising slowness to her waist and hips, moulding her against the hard length of him until she could feel every bone, every inch of his tautly muscled thighs.

Her skin was tender where the sun had burnt, but such was the desire that flamed through her nerve stream that she ignored it, wanting more than anything to cling even closer, to run her fingers through the sensual black hair, feel the shape of his head beneath her palms.

But good sense told her that this was exactly what he expected. She must escape before she lost control. With a strength born of desperation she struggled violently in his arms, straining to free herself.

With a harsh ejaculation he let her go, and even in the artificial light of the lamps Susi could see that his face had paled, tight lines of pain accentuating the angles of his jaw.

Immediately she realised that he had thought her reason for withdrawing was because she found him repulsive. 'You were hurting my back,' she said defensively, sorrowfully. There was a stillness about him that was frightening. 'My sunburn—it's very tender.'

'A convenient excuse!' he slammed, glaring angrily before striding away towards the house.

Susi watched him sadly. Scars or not, he was a sensually virile male animal—a type she had never met before. The impact of his kiss had been mind-shattering—an experience she would not forget in a hurry. Her involuntary reaction to his overpowering maleness had been unexpected, her nerves still tingled, and she did not know why.

Eventually she made her way back to her room, sitting near the window, looking out at the star-studded sky, at the crescent of moon; listening to the ceaseless chirr of a million crickets, to the higher-pitched tones of the cicadas.

She wished her thoughts were as peaceful as the night. She was disturbed by Latham's reaction. He had a chip on his shoulder as big as a plank of wood—and she had not helped.

Her horror on seeing his scars had not been because of the mess the horse's hooves had made of his chest, but because it was her brother who had caused it. It made her feel she wanted to disown Carl. It was a mean thing to have done. Latham had in no way deserved that.

She tried to recall Carl as she had known him. With

the ten-year gap between them he had never been much of a companion. He had used her, making her fetch and carry, and he had teased her mercilessly, but she could not recall him being vindictive. She supposed that in his own way he had been fond of her, but he had been a remote figure and when he emigrated she had not really missed him.

Her parents had, though, and it was because of them that she knew she must still try to find him. She had to tell him about their accident—and she could also tackle him about what he had done to Latham Elliot.

Not that it would help Latham, nothing would help now, but if Carl apologised maybe it would ease the pain? It was worth a try anyway.

A tap on her bedroom door disturbed her thoughts. Before she could answer it was pushed open and Latham Elliot walked inside. His trunks were replaced by close-fitting black corduroy pants, and a sleeveless black vest hid the disfiguring scars. But Susi could not forget them. Their total unexpectedness would be with her for a long time.

Her heart jolted now at the sight of him, making her angry with herself for responding to a man who had no interest in her. Latham had shut himself off from the whole world. He would never let any woman near him again. She must harden her heart, forget he was a sexually attractive male—the first one ever to make her feel purely feminine. 'How dare you come into my room without being asked!'

'I've brought some lotion for your sunburn. It's specially formulated to ease the sting. Take off your top, I'll do your back.' Although the tight lines had gone his eyes remained cold and hard. He made no effort to disguise the fact that he was still offended.

Susi stared incredulously, her pulses throbbing with

anger—or was it excitement at the thought of this sexy man's hands on her body? 'You have a cheek! I appreciate your thoughtfulness, but I'll do it myself, thank you.' She held out her hand.

He smiled grimly. 'Don't be pathetically prim. I have no intention of ever trying to make love to you again. You've proved conclusively what I guessed all along.' He shook the bottle and poured some of the contents into his palm. 'Come along, my patience is running thin.'

'If you have any at all,' muttered Susi, begrudgingly stripping off her cotton tee-shirt and turning her back resolutely on him, flinching as the cold lotion touched her skin.

Latham drew in a swift angry breath and she knew at once what he was thinking. God, it was so easy to upset him—but useless to try and reassure him that she meant nothing at all by her involuntary movement.

But when he unfastened her bra with one quick deft movement then she did react, crossing her arms defensively in front of her and grating savagely through her teeth, 'Is that necessary?'

'Very,' he replied coldly, 'if I'm to do the job properly. Keep still, will you? It's not a novelty seeing a woman's naked breasts. They mean nothing to me.' He met her eyes through the mirror on the opposite wall.

Hers were a vivid startling green, but his were as black as night—and completely devoid of expression. He could not have put her down more efficiently had he thrown a bucket of cold water over her. Thank you very much, she thought, I need you like I need a dose of salts.

'I suppose——' her voice was thick with temper, 'that at one time you had difficulty in fighting women off?' She did not care now whether she hurt him. He had hurt her, and it was imperative she fight back.

His hands stilled and Susi felt the tension bite through him, saw the flare of pain in his eyes. 'I've had my fair share.' The admission leapt from his strangled throat.

'And now you're immune to us?'

'Yes!' It was a harsh confession. 'What point is there in being otherwise?'

'I think you're being unnecessarily hard on yourself.' Susi knew she was braving his anger, but what had she to lose? 'You're not giving yourself the chance to find out. Have you been out with any girls since your—er—accident?'

'I don't have to,' he grated. 'I know.'

His fingers bit into her shoulder and Susi knew he did not even realise he was hurting. She could feel the imprint of each one of them, knew that tomorrow she would be bruised. 'You know nothing. It's all in your mind.'

Through the mirror their eyes met yet again. '*In my mind?* Just look at me. Tell me I'm imagining what your brother did. My God, I wish he was here now!' His hard fingers moved from her shoulders to her throat, pressing with sudden savage intensity. 'I'd kill him!'

Against her back Susi felt the hammer beats of his heart, the heat of his powerful body, and was afraid. 'You're sick,' she cried, struggling to free herself. 'You can't lay all the blame on Carl. I'm sure he never meant to do that to you.'

'Didn't he?' The thick brows rose in a crooked line. 'That's all you know. When a man's likely to be slung into jail—again—there's no saying what he will do.'

Susi's green eyes widened disbelievingly and she moistened her suddenly dry lips with the tip of her tongue. 'What do you mean, *again?*' It was as though someone was crushing her chest, forcing all the air out of her lungs.

'It wasn't the first time he'd been in trouble.' Latham spun her round to face him, holding her against the rock hardness of his chest, compelling her to look into the powerful blackness of his eyes. 'I knew that when I took him on. But I was prepared to give him a chance. It was the biggest mistake I ever made.' Again his fingers bit mercilessly into her.

'You're lying!' Every pulse in Susi's body throbbed. Even the blood pounded in her head. She felt as though she was going to pass out. Carl, a criminal? It couldn't be. There had to be something wrong.

'It's true. If you imagined him to be some little plaster saint then you're in for a big shock. He has a string of minor convictions as long as your arm. The last time he got into trouble he was jailed for six months. It was after that that I took him on. No one else would have him.' Latham's lips were bloodless, bared against his teeth, the scar standing out in jagged relief against the paleness of his skin.

Susi stared up at him with wide haunted eyes, for once glad of the arms that bound her. She was on the verge of collapse, her legs feeling as though her bones had melted. 'I won't believe you, I won't.' But there was no conviction in her voice.

'You have no option.'

She shook her head weakly. 'Not Carl. Not my own brother. He wouldn't do a——' Then she paused, and something that had puzzled her many years ago suddenly began to make sense.

She could have been no more than four or five at the time, but now she recalled the big red-faced policeman who came to their house. There had been a lot of grave talking and Carl had been in disgrace for a long time afterwards. When she asked what it was about no one would tell her, but very often Susi had seen her mother red-eyed from crying. She had forgotten all about it until now.

'Having second thoughts?' Latham's thickly sarcastic voice bit into her reflection.

'I remembered something,' she admitted reluctantly.

'That made you think it was not such an improbable situation?'

She nodded, compressing her lips, her eyes deeply unhappy. 'What did he do, all those other times when he was in trouble?'

He shrugged. 'Petty thieving, usually on a small scale, and always from his employers. He's a bad lot, make no mistake about that. I've never seen a man so crazed as he was that day he drove Black Knight at me. He's blown the one chance he's ever likely to get. No one else will employ him, I've made sure of that. His name's blacklisted in the whole of New South Wales, throughout Australia in fact, and if I ever get hold of him——'

He looked down at her and seemed suddenly to realise that she was still half naked. 'Make yourself decent,' he said thickly, thrusting her from him.

Susi swallowed painfully and with hands that trembled pulled on her thin tee-shirt, aware that it strained across her breasts, that her nipples were hard and erect from contact with Latham's body. Not that it had any effect on him. She doubted whether he would even flicker an eyelash if she stood naked and offered herself to him. At this moment his interest in women was nil.

Nor was she particularly concerned whether he thought her desirable or not. Her main thoughts were with Carl. Her own brother a criminal! It did not bear thinking about. How thankful she was that her parents had never found out. He had always written such glowing letters home, boasting how well he was doing. They had never for one moment doubted that he had made a new start.

His letters must have stopped when he was serving his prison sentence—and after that he had been too ashamed to write.

She ought to have guessed that there was something wrong when she discovered he had left his Sydney flat. The strange look that his one-time neighbour had given her, the secret smile when she disclosed where he worked. It was probably common knowledge that he had been in prison.

And what did that make her? Was the stigma attached to her too? Latham Elliot seemed to think he had the right to keep her here to pay her brother's debts. The whole situation was becoming vastly unreal.

'I must find Carl,' she said breathlessly, her chest heaving as she fought to control her emotions. 'I must talk to him. He needs help.'

'Help!' Latham spat the word in disgust. 'He's beyond help. I gave him every chance under the sun—and what did he do? It wasn't as though he didn't earn a decent wage, he didn't need to steal. The trouble with him was he liked drink and women too much.'

'I would still like to find him,' she said quietly. 'He at least should be told that our parents are—dead.'

Fractionally, only fractionally, his face softened. 'You took it hard? And now you've discovered your brother's no good either? Life's not very fair, is it? Is he all the family you have?'

She nodded. 'Both my parents were only children—and there was just Carl and myself. I suppose I have some distant relatives somewhere, but none that I'm in touch with. I want Carl.'

His face tightened. 'So do I. Perhaps it might be a good idea to let you find him. You can bring him to me.'

'So that you can take the law into your own hands?' flung Susi incautiously. 'No, thank you! If I find my brother I shall make sure that you two never meet.'

'I don't think there's much chance of you finding him,' said Latham smoothly. 'He'll have put as much distance between me and him as possible. I wouldn't be surprised if he hasn't skipped the country.'

'Oh!' Susi had not thought of that. She eyed Latham anxiously. 'What if he's gone home? I couldn't bear for him to find out from a stranger about Mum and Dad.'

He took her shoulders and this time there was no savagery in his actions. 'Seriously, I don't think he'd have done that. Air fares aren't cheap, he'd never be able to save up enough money. No, he's still in Australia somewhere. But the best you can do is forget him, Susi. He's not worth breaking your heart over.'

It was the first time he had called her Susi and she looked at him with wide pain-filled eyes. 'Have you any brothers or sisters, Mr Elliot?'

He shook his head.

'I thought not,' she said intensely. 'You have no idea how I feel. You're inhuman when it comes to other people's feelings. You're so busy feeling sorry for yourself you don't care about anyone else!'

His fingers became pincer-like again, his face all angles and drawn skin, a muscle jerking spasmodically in his jaw. 'When I want your opinion of me I'll ask for it.'

Susi twisted free and glared. 'I think it's time you went,' she muttered through barely parted lips.

There was black menace in his eyes as he studied her for several tense seconds. Susi had the feeling he would love to get his fingers round her throat and squeeze every ounce of life from her. She was reminding him too vividly of the man who had scarred him for life.

Carl and herself both had the same auburn hair and unusual grey-green eyes. His face was long and strong-boned, whereas her own was softer and rounder, but there was no mistaking they were brother and sister.

Latham was doing himself no good keeping her here. The mental torture must surely be greater than his satisfaction in trying to make her suffer?

She wished she could break the contact between them, but there was something hypnotic in the way he was looking at her, his eyes blazing with an emotion she could not understand. He had her under his spell as surely as if she was bound with ropes of steel.

It was Latham himself who suddenly swung away, his nostrils flaring, lips grim and compressed. 'If you still have any notion about going after that hare-brained brother of yours, forget it,' he hissed through his teeth. 'You'll not leave Kalabara until I say so!'

If anything was calculated to make Susi fight this was it. 'I don't think, Mr Elliot, that if I really made up my mind you would be able to stop me. As it happens, I'm quite content here for the moment.'

'Why?'

The suddenness of his question took her by surprise. She wondered whether she dared admit that he himself was the attraction? He was one hell of a man, hiding for the moment beneath a tough veneer—a skin put there by her crook of a brother. She wanted to find out what lay beneath that façade. He intrigued her like no one else ever had.

Up till now she had had no time for men, not in a physical sense. Because she had carved a career for herself in a man's world she had had to grow her own

protective skin. She countered all advances with cold
indifference until gradually her colleagues had accepted
her as one of them. She knew they respected her for not
using her sex to her advantage. She wanted no favours,
and expected none. So far as she was concerned she was
their equal.

But no way was she Latham Elliot's equal, and he
was making sure she knew that. He intended
subjugating her whether she liked it or not. She met his
eyes with a calm she was far from feeling. What woman
in her right mind could look at a man as sexy as
Latham Elliot and not be affected? His scar added
rather than detracted from his appeal; it gave him a
warrior-like appearance, made him look tougher, more
virile—if that were possible.

Her pulses hammered as she spoke. 'You have a
beautiful home, Mr Elliot, in a beautiful country. Far
from feeling that I'm being punished—for a crime I
haven't committed—I feel that I'm on holiday.'

'In that case,' he ground bitterly, 'I shall have to
think of something else for you to do. Something to fill
in those long hours you would otherwise spend by my
pool.'

Her chin jerked and she was ready with a heated
retort, but already he had spun on his heel and strode
from the room, the door shuddering on its hinges as he
banged it behind him.

CHAPTER THREE

Susi took the first opportunity that presented itself to speak to Jake. She had a feeling he might know something about her brother. He was a man who rarely volunteered information but was quite willing to talk when she drew him on.

Usually Latham was the last to leave the breakfast table, but this morning he disappeared before any of the men, causing a few raised eyebrows, and it was the old man who remained after the others had gone.

'Jake,' said Susi, sliding on to the bench beside him, 'where do you think Carl has gone?'

He gave her a quick look, his pale watery blue eyes both anxious and puzzled at the same time. 'What makes you think I might know?'

'It's just a feeling I have,' shrugged Susi. 'Someone has to know where he is.'

'When Carl left here we didn't see his heels for dust. I'd like to help, but I don't see how I can. I know he's your brother, but he's as unlike you as—I am from Latham.' There was a wry smile on his dried-up lips.

'That doesn't mean I don't love him,' said Susi quietly. 'I tried to explain this to Latham, but he won't listen. He keeps telling me that Carl's a bad lot and I'm better off without him. But blood is thicker than water. Can you understand that?'

Jake nodded as he slowly packed his pipe with tobacco and took several long pulls before he was satisfied it was alight. When he was wreathed in smoke

51

he said, 'I've a family of my own and good or bad I still love 'em. I do understand, but you're asking the wrong one. In fact I don't think there's anyone on this farm who could tell you where Carl is at this moment. It wouldn't be safe for him to show his face. Not only is Latham after his blood, but every single man who works here too. They didn't like what he did. I sure wouldn't like to be in his shoes.'

'I don't like what he's done either,' said Susi, 'but I can help him, I know I can. I'm not his kid sister any longer, I'm a woman. He needs someone who cares, someone to look after him, make sure he doesn't do anything wrong again.'

One gnarled hand closed over hers. 'He doesn't deserve you, Susi. If you'd been out here with him I reckon none of this would have happened. He's run wild.'

'There you are, you see.' Susi took the horny hand between her own soft fingers. 'Please, Jake, think hard. There has to be someone who knows where he's likely to be.'

Jake heaved a sigh, a slow sad smile creasing his face. 'I'll ask around. I'm not promising, mind. Most people keep their mouths shut where anything like this is concerned. They don't want to get involved.'

With that Susi had to be content.

Lunchtime came and went and she thought Latham had forgotten his threat. It was not until she was changing ready for another session in the pool that she heard his gravelly voice calling her name.

Pulling back on the cotton dress she had just discarded, Susi made her way in the direction of his voice, finding him in the doorway to his study. He filled the frame with his bulk and she noted, not for the first time, that he always managed to turn the scarred side of

his face away from her. She wished he wouldn't. It
made no difference.

But he would not thank her for telling him, so she
followed meekly into the room. 'Can you type?' he
asked abruptly, his face as unemotional as it had been
the night before, his black eyes just as damning.

She eyed him coldly. 'Since when has typing been
part of an engineer's education?'

His eyes narrowed dangerously. 'I'm asking the
questions.'

Susi shrugged with pretended indifference, something
she was far from feeling. Even in this difficult mood
Latham still exuded a sexual magnetism that she found
difficult to ignore. 'As a matter of fact, yes, I can. I
considered it a useful skill.'

'Good,' he answered crisply. 'I have a pile of letters
here that need answering. I was going to do them
myself—I've scribbled notes on each one of them. Do
you think you could manage that?'

'I can do most things I set my mind to,' said Susi
with equal aggression. 'But I don't see why I should.
Why don't you hire a secretary?'

'Because I don't want any females at Kalabara,' he
snapped savagely. 'Surely you can understand that?'

'There are male secretaries.' Susi's eyes were flashing
green, a sure sign that her temper was getting the better
of her. 'You have no right to put all this work on me—
I'm entitled to some spare time.'

'You're entitled to nothing,' he snarled. 'You're here
to do exactly what I tell you. You're paying Carl's
debts—don't ever forget that.'

A thrill of excitement coursed through her veins. The
tension between them was electric, though she doubted
Latham was reacting to her in the same way. His
sexuality seemed to leap out at her, more especially

when he was angry. Her heart began to beat painfully fast.

Nevertheless she managed to say bitterly, 'I hardly think you're likely to let me. But I suppose you may as well show me where everything is.' There seemed no way she was going to get out of it.

She followed him to his big desk near the window. The portable typewriter was already in position and no sooner had he explained everything than he had gone.

Left alone, Susi sat a moment before beginning to type, finding it difficult to imagine Latham's big fingers using these delicate keys.

She had been in this room often when doing the cleaning. It was stamped with Latham's personality and smelled heavily of the cheroots that he smoked. The walls were wood-panelled and hung with framed pictures of various racehorses that his stallions had sired.

One wall was filled with books, most of them about horses, some about the Australian Outback, the aboriginals, some about wild life not only in Australia but different countries of the world.

Latham was very much an outdoor man, and it surprised her that he should do his paperwork himself. She supposed it had been a relief when Carl helped. It was a pity her brother had abused that trust. He could have done very well for himself.

Surprisingly she found pleasure in typing his letters. An office career was something she had scorned, feeling the routine would be dull, but today she found it extremely interesting. Most of the letters were enquiries from people wishing to bring their mares for covering.

The stud was run on a very strict and tight schedule.

Nothing was left to chance. Everything was organised down to the last detail. There was one letter congratulating him on the way he had handled a particularly truculent mare, with a promise of half share in the first winnings if the filly should prove as successful a racer as her mother. Latham had indicated that he wished the money to be donated to a charity of their own choice. Susi was surprised by his generosity.

Not all the letters were connected with the stud farm. She discovered that he had other interests—a sheep farm at Bourke, part shares in an opal mine at Lightning Ridge. He really must be a very rich man.

But obviously horses were in his blood. He was never more happy than when he was outside with them. Even now he was leading one of the stallions from the stable, saddling him, springing into the saddle with an ease that came of a lifetime doing just that.

He sat the horse well, and it was a few minutes before Susi realised she had stopped typing in order to feast her eyes on him, although it was not until she turned her attention back to the typewriter that she discovered she was trembling.

She was seeing Latham in a way she had never noticed any man before. He was getting beneath her skin, despite the aggressive way he treated her. She could no longer ignore that strong masculine body, those long powerful limbs, the sensuality that set her pulses racing. He was easily the most intoxicating man she had ever met.

It was disappointing to discover that she would not have time to finish the letters before cooking their evening meal. She had wanted to impress him with her efficiency. But he would certainly not be impressed if there was no food before him when he had finished his day's work! Her father had always said that the way to

a man's heart was through his stomach—and her
mother had been a Cordon Bleu cook, so he should
know.

Susi supposed she could be grateful her mother had
insisted she learn to cook too, otherwise she would
never have made a success of the job that had been
thrust upon her now. She had never expected her
culinary skills to be put to the test quite so exactingly.
Not that the hands wanted anything fancy. Something
plain, basic and filling was the order of the day—giant-
sized steaks or thick succulent chops with plenty of
potatoes and vegetables.

For the next few days Susi was kept so busy she had
no time to think about Latham, Carl or anything else.
But then one morning Jake came to her in the kitchen
as she worked. Susi looked at him wearily, wiping her
hair from her face with the back of her hand.

'You're doing too much.' His kind old face creased in
a frown of concern.

'I don't mind,' said Susi. 'The work stops me
thinking about Carl.'

'Humph!' grunted the old man. 'Much as I admire
Latham I don't think he has any right to make you pay
off Carl's debts like this. It isn't your fault he's a bad
'un. Latham has his mind twisted somewhere—and
you're a mug for giving in. Why do you do it?'

Susi shrugged. 'I suppose you wouldn't believe me if I
said I enjoyed it?'

'I wouldn't,' agreed Jake tightly.

Susi grinned ruefully. 'It is the truth. I'm not saying
I'd enjoy it if it was permanent.' There was laughter in
her voice. 'But at the moment it's a novelty.'

'A novelty, eh? It seems to me like you're trying to
prove to Latham that he can't put you down no matter
how hard he tries.'

'I didn't realise I was so obvious,' admitted Susi. 'But I'm sure you're not here to discuss that. Have you any news about Carl?'

Her voice was eager, but Jake pulled a wry face. 'I have the address of a girl who could help. It'll be worth a try anyway.'

Susi was elated. She wrapped her arms about him and planted a kiss on his leathery cheek, putting the slip of paper into her pocket. 'I love you, Jake. You're a darling!'

He looked embarrassed. 'You deserve a break,' he said gruffly. 'I just hope you know what you're doing. If Latham finds out I've given you that address he'll skin me alive.'

For the rest of the morning Susi debated how to get away from Kalabara. The girl's address was in Sydney. She wondered whether Latham would swallow the excuse that she needed to do some personal shopping, or if he would think she was planning to run away.

After lunch, when Latham stopped behind to smoke his customary cheroot, she approached him, her heart skidding along at twice its normal rate, her eyes over-bright, warm colour flooding her cheeks. She looked guilty before she had even put her question. 'I'd like to go into Sydney—I need to do some shopping. Can I borrow your car?'

His brows knit together and he observed her suspiciously through the thin haze of smoke that surrounded him. Susi felt her nerves quiver at the directness of his gaze. There had been little direct contact between the two of them during these last few days. When he wanted to tell her anything he left messages on the desk.

'How do I know,' he asked stiffly, 'that you will return? I could lose my car—and you.'

She eyed him coldly. 'You'll just have to trust me.'

'That's something I'm not prepared to do.' His black eyes had never been more formidable.

Susi turned away. 'You're a hard man, Mr Elliot.'

'I happen to know you'd do anything to try and find that brother of yours. Your excuses don't fool me.'

'Looking for Carl in Sydney would be like looking for a needle in a haystack, as you well know,' she cried angrily. 'I'm under no delusion that he's still there. All I want to do is some shopping.'

'In that case,' said Latham, 'I'll take you myself.'

Susi's eyes shot wide. It would ruin everything. He would not let her out of his sight. 'There's no need,' she said, trying to make herself sound calm. 'I give you my word I'll come back.'

'A Kingswood word?' he asked scathingly, thick brows rising in absolute mockery. 'Either I take you or you don't go at all. The choice is yours.'

'I'm not a liar, Mr Elliot,' she said strongly. 'But you leave me no alternative.' Maybe she would find some way of giving him the slip. She must find this girl's address and see if she knew where Carl was. It was too much to expect that he might be living with her, but she might at least get a lead.

'Tomorrow, then,' he said crisply. 'We'll go as soon as the men have had their breakfast. Jake can cook lunch.'

Throughout the rest of the day Susi could do nothing but think of the forthcoming trip. Searching through Latham's books she found a street plan of Sydney and discovered that Alison Cordell lived not far from the city centre. It might be easier than she had expected. He could not keep his eye on her the whole of the time. She would take her opportunity the moment it presented itself.

She did not see him again until breakfast. Beneath her overall she wore a cotton sundress in palest lemon which complemented the slight tan she had acquired. Not that she had had much time for sunbathing, but even so the few minutes she snatched had transformed her normal ivory skin to a delicate shade of honey.

As soon as the men left the kitchen Latham asked her abruptly how long it would take her to get ready. Susi whisked off her enveloping wrap, revealing the crisp dress. 'I'm ready now,' she announced. 'Just give me a minute to get my bag.'

It pleased her to see the flicker of surprise in his black eyes. No doubt he was used to his women taking hours to get ready, but she had never felt the need to impress a man and she had no intention of starting on Latham Elliot, no matter that he set her pulses racing in a way no one else ever had.

When she gave her appearance a final check in her room she realised it had been a mistake to coil up her hair. It revealed far too plainly the long slender column of her throat, accentuated the gentle rise of her breasts above the low-cut bodice. Her eyes were over-bright, her cheeks flushed, and although she tried to convince herself it was because there was a chance she might trace Carl, she was under no delusion that most of her excitement was caused by anticipation of Latham's company for the next few hours. As an afterthought she added gold hoops to her ears, then snatched them out again angrily. Latham would not even notice. She must never forget that he had lost all interest in women.

His car was long, sleek and silver-blue, a bench seat at the front, the gears automatic. Susi was grateful for the empty space between her and this excitingly sensual male animal.

He drove down the mile-long rough track, neither of them speaking until they reached the smooth tarmac road. She was vitally conscious of the long powerful legs stretched out in front of him, of the hard-boned hands on the wheel.

Her whole body responded to Latham's masculinity. The spicy odour of his aftershave, combined with the inevitable smell of horses and cigars, intoxicated her and in the close confines of the car there was no escaping his total, devastating magnetism.

'Do you go into Sydney often?' she asked, more to break the silence than any real desire to know. Sitting so close to Latham was like being in front of an open fire. Although the car was air-conditioned it made no difference. Already her hands were clammy, her mouth uncomfortably dry.

He glanced across. His scar was away from her and there was no denying that he was an exceedingly attractive man. He was not handsome in the true sense of the word, but his rugged strong face could not be ignored. He was as potent as neat alcohol, and she wanted to reach out and touch him.

So strong was the feeling that Susi locked her fingers together, an action that did not go unnoticed by Latham. 'There was no need for you to put yourself out for me,' she said, when he did not answer.

'Don't worry, I haven't.' The black eyes had never been more caustic. 'I have business to attend to, otherwise you would never have been allowed out.'

'You're a swine!' raged Susi. 'You have no right punishing me for what my brother has done!' Her warm feelings evaporated as quickly as they had come.

'Something tells me that you're enjoying it,' said

Latham surprisingly. 'I've not had one word of complaint no matter how much work I pile on you. If it really went against the grain you'd soon tell me, I know that. You don't strike me as the type to take anything sitting down.'

Susi eyed him coldly. 'I really don't see how you can have formed such an opinion.'

His lips curled in a humourless smile. 'You'd be surprised, Susi, exactly what I think of you.'

Her eyes grew wide. 'Perhaps you'd care to enlighten me?'

'No, thanks,' he growled. 'Only time will tell whether I'm right.'

They drove for a few more miles in complete silence, Susi trying to concentrate on the landscape, eyeing the various farm buildings they passed, the thirsty gum trees, the arid pastures. A few wild flowers struggled to survive, scrawny cattle searched for blades of grass. Everywhere was so dry. Their car churned up dust along the road and Susi thought of green England.

But it was difficult to keep her attention on anything other than the man at her side. He dominated her thoughts entirely. It was a big car, but they could have been squashed together for all the difference it made. She was chokingly aware of his presence, not surprised when she found it difficult to breathe.

'Have you any music in this car?' she asked, her voice husky with emotion.

Latham's lips quirked almost as though he knew exactly what she was thinking. He reached out and turned a switch, and immediately the car was filled with the strident tones of a current pop group.

He turned it so loud that conversation was impossible. It suited Susi—anything to block out the devastating presence of this man.

When they neared the suburbs Latham needed all his concentration to negotiate the heavy traffic which Susi knew they would now be in until they reached the city centre. He lowered the radio and manouevred the big car in and out of the rushing traffic.

Susi had no fears for her safety. He was completely at home behind the wheel, confident in every move he made. Even when he braked suddenly because a car stopped dead in front of him, and Susi's seatbelt jerked her back in her seat, she did not bat an eyelid. Her confidence in Latham was supreme. She surprised herself, for normally she was a nervous passenger.

When they reached the city centre and the cars were nose to tail in a maze that Susi thought no one could ever get out of, he knew exactly where he was going. In no time at all he had parked the car and they were walking along Castlereagh Street.

'Exactly where is it you want to go?' asked Latham. 'Centre Point is as good a place as any if it's modern shops you're after. Or there are some quaint arcades where you can buy souvenirs and gifts. Although if you were telling me the truth that's not the sort of thing you're looking for.'

'I wouldn't mind looking around while I am here,' said Susi. 'The day I arrived I did no more than go straight to Carl's flat and then get a taxi to your place. I saw nothing of Sydney. It would be a pity to go back without seeing any of the sights.'

'I agree,' he said surprisingly. 'But we'll do your shopping first, then I'll give you a guided tour. Not that you can see much in a day—you really need to spend at least a week to see what Australia's Leading Lady has to offer.'

No way was he going to let her go off on her own, thought Susi, her heart plummeting. 'I thought you said you had business to attend to?'

Those black eyes looked at her suspiciously, seeing right through into her mind. 'I have an insurance problem to sort out, that's all. You can come with me.'

'I'd much rather browse around on my own,' said Susi quickly. 'I can't imagine you enjoy the same sort of shops as me. I thought I'd buy a couple of sundresses and some shorts. I'm sure you'd be bored looking at things like that.'

'Would I?' His brows rose in a mocking curve and he dropped an arm carelessly about her shoulders. 'Would I, Susi? How little you know me. I think I'd find it most interesting, especially if you model them for me.'

His touch was electric, searing her skin like a red-hot poker, and she shook herself free. He laughed softly and she hated him at that moment. He knew exactly what he was doing. Getting away from Latham was going to be more difficult than she had expected.

They trailed from store to store, Susi buying things she did not need, all the time keeping her eye open for an opportunity to slip away.

Her chance came when they were in the insurance building. He explained his problem over the counter but was invited to go through to see the manager. He turned to Susi. 'Come, we shan't be long.'

But she declined. 'I'll wait here.' And there was nothing he could do in front of a room full of strangers. The expression in his coal-black eyes warned her in no mean terms that if she left she would be in trouble.

No sooner was he out of sight than Susi raced down the stairs and out into the street, hailing a passing taxi. She gave him Alison Cordell's address and in no time at all was being whisked through the streets. She paid him as soon as they arrived, it never occurring to her that the girl might not be in.

She rang the bell impatiently several times before accepting that this was the case. Taking a slip of paper from her bag, she scribbled a message asking Alison to let her know Carl's address if she knew it, stating how important it was that she get hold of him. She gave Latham Elliot's address, feeling sure he would not open her mail. Whatever else she thought of him she did not doubt his integrity.

There was nothing for it then but to make her way back to the insurance office and hope that Latham was still there, not that she expected it—nor was he. She must have been away almost an hour. Neither could she remember where the car was, which was stupid, but not surprising in this strange city.

So she went to the Opera House and took the guided tour round the five theatres and various halls, sitting later in one of the restaurants, enjoying a delicious piece of pavlova and a cup of coffee. It was a most unusual and impressive building, designed, she was informed, by Danish architect Joern Utzon and completed in 1973 at a cost of a hundred and two million dollars.

Outside she watched the ferries chugging from Circular Quay to their various destinations across the harbour, the hydrofoil skimming the blue, blue water, the yachts with their sails like brilliant butterflies. And she wandered through the streets, finding herself once again in Centre Point.

She took the lift up Sydney Tower to the Observation level. The views here were out of this world. The unique shape of Sydney Harbour could not be seen from the land, but from this vantage point it revealed its countless inlets and creeks in all their glory.

The Opera House looked for all the world like a

convoluted shell, the Harbour Bridge exactly like the coathanger the Australians endearingly called it, the bobbing yachts mere toys from this height.

In another direction she coud see tall office blocks, Barclays Bank, the insurance building where she had given Latham the slip. As she moved around she spied in the distance the airport where she had landed not so many days ago. It seemed a lifetime.

And further round still the Blue Mountains about which she had heard so much, and which one day she would like to visit. Although it seemed unlikely, with Latham keeping her virtually under lock and key.

At length she decided it was time to find her way back to Kalabara, and reluctant though she was to spend her money on a taxi yet again it was by far the most convenient way of getting there. She was standing on the edge of the pavement, eagerly looking for a taxi with a vacant sign on its roof, when Latham's big blue car screamed to a full stop in front of her.

She slid inside, casting a wary glance at him, not surprised to see the tight lines of his face, the grim jaw and cold black eyes. 'Where the hell did you go?' he asked grimly, swerving out into the line of traffic, ignoring the horns which blared all around him.

Susi shrugged with pretended indifference. 'I got bored waiting for you. I've been looking around. I went up Sydney Tower and into the Opera House. It really is a fantastic place, it's like walking inside a sea-shell. There's an organ concert there next month I'd like to go to.'

'Don't give me that garbage!' flung Latham nastily. 'I know where you've been. I knew that was why you wanted to come here. A waste of time, wasn't it? You won't find him in Sydney, he's too afraid for his own hide.'

'I've not been looking for Carl,' cried Susi adamantly. 'And that's the truth, whether you believe it or not.'

It was clear he did not believe her. The hard look in those eyes was sceptical in the extreme. 'You have no other reason to run away.'

'I happen to like looking around on my own,' she protested. 'But I wasn't running away from the stud. As a matter of fact I was hailing a taxi when you picked me up. I was going back.'

He looked at her doubtfully. 'You can tell me all the lies you like, Susi, I shan't accept them. But make no mistake, I shan't let you out of my sight again. Not until I consider your debt paid.'

'Which will be never, by the look of it,' complained Susi angrily. 'I don't mind working for you, I freely admit that, but I do object to being kept a prisoner. There's really no need—I'm not likely to run away.'

'If I make it too easy for you it will be no penance,' said Latham arrogantly, 'and when you've discovered where your brother is it will be goodbye. Don't think I can't see through you. You know which side your bread's buttered. So far as you're concerned you're getting a free roof over your head and doing everything you can to trace Carl's whereabouts at the same time. But believe me, you won't get anywhere—I won't let you. There's no way I would help a Kingswood.'

'You can't tar us both with the same brush!' Susi's aggression flared, her eyes grew wild.

'I'm not doing that.' Latham's eyes were as hard as polished jet. 'I'm merely trying to make you see sense.'

'You'll never do that,' she burst out. 'He's my brother—he's the only family I have. One way or another I intend to find him.'

His face hardened. 'Don't forget that I'm gunning for him too. You could be doing yourself a bad turn.'

'*If* I find him, I shall certainly warn him about you.' Susi's tones were bitter. 'It is not my intention to put his life in danger. The sensible thing to do, if you ever did meet, would be to talk the whole thing over. I'm sure it could be resolved.'

His fingers tightened on the wheel, knuckles gleaming like ivory. 'You have no idea what you're talking about. By your own admittance your brother is a stranger to you. Let him stay that way. I could never speak civilly to a man who's tried to take my life.'

Susi shook her head angrily. 'This whole conversation is getting us nowhere. It's pointless. I don't want to discuss him with you any more.'

'*You* don't want to discuss him? You were the one who brought the whole thing up again by disappearing as you did. What else was I supposed to think? What other reason had you for going off on your own?'

Susi compressed her lips. 'I'd rather not discuss it. The whole situation is intolerable.'

'I agree,' he rapped. 'Carl Kingswood's name leaves a nasty taste in my mouth. The less I hear of him the better.'

'In that case,' said Susi coldly, 'I would have thought the less you saw of me the better too. I can't see what you're hoping to achieve by keeping me at Kalabara. Unless it's cheap labour you're after. Is that it?' She was finding it difficult to breathe, dragging in air hungrily through tortured lungs.

'I don't regard you as cheap, Susi.' The biting anger in his voice made her look at him sharply. 'You've cost me one hell of a lot. At least that bastard brother of yours has, and so far as I'm concerned that includes you too.'

She turned her head away, swallowing a sudden galling lump in her throat. Latham Elliot was so unreasonable! No matter what she said it made no difference, she might as well keep her mouth shut.

Not until they had left the city of Sydney behind did she begin to relax and take more interest in her surroundings than she had done so far. They passed through various towns, each with its main street of shops, the pavements shaded with one long continuous canopy.

Most people wore shorts and skinny tops, their skins tanned to varying shades of brown. It was a real outdoor life here and she could understand her brother enjoying it so much. When he first wrote home he had enthused over the barbecues and the bush-walking. It was certainly very different from England.

Several kilometres farther on she caught tantalising glimpses of the ocean, of foaming surf on almost white beaches. Her eyes were bright as she turned involuntarily to Latham. 'I didn't realise we were so close to the sea. Could we go and have a look, do you think?'

'There's a beach a few kilometres away from Kalabara.' He looked amused at her enthusiasm. 'We'll go there, if you like, but first I thought I'd show you the Blowhole at Kiama. It's quite spectacular when it's blowing properly. It's a rough sea today with the wind south-east. Conditions are perfect.'

This was the first offer of friendship, if it could be called that, that he had extended towards her. He seemed to have got over his black mood. She smiled. 'I don't profess to know what a blowhole is, but yes, I'd love to see it.'

As they neared Kiama he explained that the rugged coastline was made of volcanic rocks. 'There are even extinct volcanoes,' he said, 'but we won't have time to examine those today. And not far away there's a tropical rain forest and Minnemurra Falls, which are certainly well worth a visit.'

Susi could not believe he was being so sociable, especially after the way he had berated her for going off on her own. But she certainly intended making the most of this unexpected opportunity.

He parked the car near the lighthouse and they made their way to the lookout. 'The sea,' explained Latham, 'is washed through that subterranean passage. It makes a tremendous noise, so be prepared.' There were several people waiting and indeed, true to form, the sea came rushing in, sending a gigantic plume of water and spray up into the air which must have been about sixty metres high. It was a spectacular sight and everyone gasped in awe, except Latham, of course, who had seen it before. He was unmoved.

Several times it blew as they watched, sometimes higher than others, and Susi wished she had her camera to capture this natural phenomenon. She turned wide shining eyes to Latham. 'It's really something, isn't it?'

He nodded, saying gruffly, 'I thought you might like it. Now I think we ought to get home—Jake will wonder what's happened to us. We'll leave the beach until another day. I don't know about you, but I'm starving.'

'Me too,' she admitted, suddenly realising that apart from the pavlova she had had nothing to eat since breakfast. It was her own fault; it had been almost lunchtime when she left Latham.

She wondered whether he had eaten, or whether he had been so disturbed by her disappearance he had not bothered with lunch either. But because of the fragile rapport that existed between them she deemed it best not to mention it.

Latham's good mood continued, and when they

arrived back at the stud he suggested they take a swim while Jake got their dinner. 'It won't hurt him to do that too.'

Susi hid her continued surprise, going to her room and putting on the brief red bikini she had worn the other day. Latham was already in the pool when she got there, and she stood and watched as his arms cleaved the water in a powerful crawl, believing he had not observed her, and was startled when he stopped and beckoned.

She dived cleanly, glad she was a good swimmer, glad of the silken coolness of the water which soothed her overheated limbs. Latham was still in an extraordinarily good humour, and they spent a quarter of an hour chasing each other, fooling about like children. Susi had never seen him like this before and was glad that he was beginning to relax with her. He was not half so self-conscious about his scars as he had been in the beginning. It was a good sign.

Latham seemed to have an inexhaustible supply of energy, professing disappointment when she declared she had had enough, catching her ankle as she hauled herself out. Unprepared, Susi lost her balance and fell back against him.

His arms bound her like steel and the next moment she found herself whipped round to face him, his mouth closing on hers as they sank like stones to the bottom of the pool.

She had never been kissed under water before and found it disturbingly erotic. Their bodies were weightless, writhing in the blue-green depths, legs and arms entwined.

He threaded his fingers through her dark hair which she had released from its braids before entering the pool, allowing its long auburn length to flow behind her like a mane, holding her head close. Not until they broke the surface did Susi realise she was desperately short of breath.

She pushed Latham away, taking deep breaths of the fragrantly perfumed evening air. But he allowed her no more than a few seconds before swooping on her mouth yet again.

His hands traced every curve of her body, holding her against him so that she could not ignore his throbbing desire. Her heart raced as she involuntarily arched herself towards him, aware of a desperate hunger within herself which matched his own.

He had been starved of a woman for so long it was as though he could contain himself no longer. He swung her into his arms and lifted her out of the pool, crushing her against his hard chest. It was then that she began to panic, realising that things might get out of hand if she did not put a stop to it. She struggled fiercely and he set her down, the moment she was free racing towards the house.

His bellow of rage followed her, but not until a heavy hand fell on her shoulder, spinning her to face him, did Susi realise that he was behind. His eyes were blazing like those of a madman. 'Why the sudden change?' he demanded harshly. 'Is it because of this?' As on that first day he jutted his jaw so that her eyes became fixed on the jagged scar running down his cheek. 'Or these?' thrusting his chest forward. 'Is it, Susi? Is it? Did you forget for a moment that I'm disfigured? My God, you sure know how to kick a man when he's down!'

Susi shook her head, her face twisted with compassion and pain for this man who was suffering unnecessarily, who felt he had a cross to bear, who refused to accept that his scars did not detract from his masculine appeal one little bit.

'No, Latham,' she said quietly. 'It's not because of them, I don't even notice them any more. They don't bother me in the slightest.'

'Then why?' he jabbed harshly. 'If you expect me to believe that, tell me why you went suddenly cold on me?'

'You frightened me,' she whispered huskily. 'You were so intense, I was out of my depth. I want to help you get over your fears, but I don't want to get— involved.'

He sneered derisively, 'I don't believe you. You sound convincing but I'm not fooled.'

Susi caught the anguish in his eyes before he swung round. 'Please, Latham,' she said softly, putting a tentative hand on his arm, 'it's not like that at all.'

'Don't touch me,' he snarled. 'Get away, for God's sake!'

'You're wrong about all this.' She tried to reason with him. 'You're too hard on yourself. You see your scars as a barrier between you and the rest of the world, but they aren't—they're nothing.'

'Nothing?' His eyes blazed furiously. 'You wouldn't say that if they were yours. Get the hell away from me, Susi, *now!*'

'I can't leave you feeling sorry for yourself.' She twisted her hands as she stood resolutely before him. 'You're not giving yourself a chance, Latham. I like you kissing me, I really do. I don't find you repulsive— nothing about you is repulsive. You were coming on a bit strong, that's all, and I'm not after an affair.'

'Who's offering you one?' he grated harshly. 'I wouldn't ask any woman to share my life ever again, even for a short time. It wouldn't be fair.'

'Then what were you after?' she demanded, her pulses racing all out of time with themselves, her breathing deep and erratic.

'It was madness,' he said thickly. 'You have no idea how desirable you are, especially in that ridiculous bikini. I can't keep my hands off you. Even now I still want you. You'd better go, before I make a complete fool of myself.'

Susi suffered agonies for him, wishing there was something she could do. 'I really meant it when I said I don't notice your scars. It's the truth, Latham, you must believe me. You're the——' she swallowed convulsively, 'the sexiest man I've ever met. No man's ever affected me the way you do.' Her admission was difficult—but if it would help, it was worth the embarrassment.

'Words are easy,' he snarled. 'It would be a different thing altogether if I really attempted to make love to you. Don't tell me your skin doesn't crawl when I touch you. Twice you've rejected me. If that doesn't tell me what you feel then nothing will.'

She shook her head in desperation. 'You've got it wrong, Latham. It's your own inferiority complex that's doing this to you. Kiss me now and I'll prove it.'

'It will prove nothing,' he bit out, throwing her a damning look from those hard black eyes. 'I made a mistake and I regret it, let's leave it at that.'

Susi felt as though she had been punched in the stomach. 'If that's what you really want?' She looked at him reproachfully with her big green eyes, before turning away and heading indoors.

Dinner was an uncomfortable meal and Susi was glad when it was over. Jake eyed the two of them curiously, but had the good sense to ask no questions. Susi felt sure Latham would have kicked him in the teeth if he had so much as dared.

Never had she met a man so difficult to get on with. She wondered if he would ever come to terms with his injury. She knew her brother had done it, but all the blame was not his. A lot was in Latham's own mind, his inability to accept that the scars made him no less of a man.

During the next few days Susi saw very little of Latham. He made sure she was kept busy, finding jobs for her that she felt sure were not necessary. Nevertheless she did not complain, needing something to fill in the long hours of each day. She began to despair of ever having a letter from Alison Cordell, unless, of course, one had arrived and Latham Elliott had held it back.

She told Jake of her escapade in Sydney, and he laughed. 'Good on you, Susi! It serves Latham right for keeping you on such a tight rein. I'm sure I don't know what's got into him. I've never known him so fanatic about anything before.'

'He's certainly making sure he gets his pound of flesh,' said Susi. 'But in actual fact I'm thriving on it. I never knew office work could be so enjoyable.'

'What is it you do, then?' asked Jake. 'I thought that was your job.'

'Didn't Latham tell you?' she laughed. 'I'm an engineer.'

The wispy brows rose in disbelief. 'You mean you fix engines, that sort of thing?'

'Not quite.' Susi could not contain her amusement. 'I'm in the electronics field, the sales side actually, but I've had to go through as thorough a training as everyone else.'

'Isn't that unusual for a woman?'

'That's what everyone says, but why shouldn't a woman do it? I reckon I'm as good as any man. I don't see why they should have the monopoly.'

'You're one of them new liberated women, then? Can't say I hold with it myself.'

Again Susi laughed. 'I expect all your wife ever did, Jake, was look after you and the kids?'

'That's right,' he nodded. 'It's what women are meant to do. But she's gone now and I look after myself.'

'Tell me,' she said impulsively, 'was Latham any different before his—accident?'

Jake shrugged, his dry old lips pulling down at the corners, adding a whole new set of lines to his wrinkled face. 'It's hard to say. Sometimes he's no different at all. On other occasions, when something happens to remind him of what Carl did, he's a difficult man. We steer clear then. I suppose he never had those black moods before. Carl did that to him. And, of course, there's no women in his life now.'

Susi nodded sadly. 'He thinks he's unattractive, repulsive, even. I've tried telling him it's all in his mind, but it makes no difference.'

'It's a pity.' Jake paused to gnaw a gnarled thumb. 'But he'll get over it given time. He's not the type to remain celibate for ever.'

On the morning following her talk with Jake, Latham was absent from the breakfast table, but waiting for her in his office when she got there. He looked in an impossibly evil mood, and Susi's stomach churned as she tried to think what she could have done.

No sooner had she walked towards the desk than he held out an envelope, shaking it furiously beneath her nose. 'What's Alison Cordell doing writing to you?'

She looked down and saw her name on the envelope. 'You've opened my mail! How dare you! Whatever comes for me here is private—you have no right to do that. Give it to me!'

He snatched it away quickly. 'I haven't opened it, Susi. I happen to know Alison's handwriting.'

'You?' she enquired, eyes narrowed. 'I thought she was a friend of my brother's?'

'She transferred her affections,' he said thickly, harshly. 'Before the accident we were on the point of getting engaged, would you believe? But then—when I was lying in hospital with my face and body swathed in bandages—she delivered her blow. She couldn't stomach being married to a disfigured man. It was goodbye, Latham, I feel sorry for you, but——' His lip curled contemptuously.

CHAPTER FOUR

SUSI shrank from the hatred on Latham's face, feeling her heart stop and then gallop at twice its normal rate. 'I didn't know,' she whispered huskily. 'I had no idea. Jake never said that——'

'Jake?' he intercepted harshly. 'What the hell's he got to do with it? Did he give you Alison's address?'

Susi nodded, realising she had said too much, hoping that by implicating the old man she was not getting him into trouble. It must have been what Jake meant when he said Latham would skin him alive if he found out. 'I asked if he could help me find Carl. He understood why it was so important to me—which is more than you did. And he said that perhaps Alison Cordell could help.'

'The hell he did!' Latham's eyes blazed. 'Jake knew she was playing around with Carl at the same time as she was seeing me, but he was too afraid of hurting me to tell me what should have been obvious to my own eyes. But he had no right sending you to her.'

'He didn't think you'd find out,' she said quietly. 'If I'd known you were going to be this upset I'd——'

'I'm not upset,' he denied loudly. 'I no longer have any feelings for that woman, except loathing. Carl's welcome to her. But I hardly think they'll still be together. He'll be too afraid I might get in touch with her, find out from her where he is. Alison probably saw him as a convenient scapegoat when she couldn't face the thought of marrying me, but I doubt it lasted. Was that where you went, that day you gave me the slip?'

Susi nodded. 'But I wasn't lying when I said I hadn't been trying to find Carl,' she added defensively.

'Indirectly you were after him,' he grated. 'I knew it had something to do with him. Why don't you open her letter and put us both out of our misery?'

Susi took the white envelope with the round black writing, turning it over and over in her hands. 'I'd rather read it when I'm alone, if you don't mind.'

'I damn well do mind,' he grated, his eyes blazing like hot coals. 'If she knows where Carl is then I have a right to know too.'

'So that you can get at him first!' burst out Susi angrily. 'Oh, no, he's my brother, Mr Elliot. I want to spend some time with him, not visit him in jail, which is where he'd end up if you got your hands on him.' She pushed the envelope into her jeans' pocket. 'I'll read it later.'

Latham bounced up and stormed over to her, his face fiercely angry. 'I respect your needs, but believe me, I intend finding out one way or another, even if it means contacting Alison myself, something I'm loath to do.'

Susie could understand that. It was this woman who had driven the stake in his heart, who had shattered his ego, made him feel that he was some kind of monster. The ironic part about it was that she had not waited to see how badly scarred he was. If she had she might have been surprised. They certainly weren't so horrific that anyone would blanch and turn away. Indeed, they made one more interested, wanting to ask questions. What had happened? How had he got them? He looked as though he must be an extremely brave man.

'I don't care what you do,' she said strongly. 'Just let me read my letter in private. If she doesn't know where he is I'll tell you, if she does, wild horses won't drag it from me.'

Their eyes met and held in one long silent hostile battle, then Latham pivoted on his heel and swung out of the room.

Susi closed the door and went over to the desk, taking the paper-knife and slitting open the envelope, surprised to find her fingers trembling as she slid out the single sheet of paper.

Dear Miss Kingswood, she read,
To say I was surprised to receive your note is putting it mildly. I didn't even know that Carl had a sister. He never told me—he never discussed his life in England. I was also most surprised to see that you're living at Kalabara. I would have thought the last person Latham Elliot would want there was you. How can you bear to look at him?
I've written and told Carl you're here, but he says he doesn't want to see you. He's afraid you'll lead Latham to him. There is no love lost between the two men, as you probably know. He suggests you go back to England and forget you ever had a brother.
Yours,
Alison Cordell

Susi read the letter through several times. It was disappointing. She refused to believe that Carl did not want to see her. Perhaps she ought to have made it quite clear that his whereabouts would remain safe with her. In no circumstances would she tell Latham Elliot. She knew exactly what this big man would do to her brother.

Neither would she return to England without seeing Carl! She wanted to tell him about their parents' fatal accident—it was too private and hurtful to put in a note.

She would ring Alison! No sooner did the thought

occur to her than she lifted down the telephone directory and began thumbing through the pages. But either Alison Cordell was not on the phone or she was ex-directory. There was no entry under her name.

The only other alternative was to visit Alison again—which could prove difficult—or write! Jake or one of the other hands would surely post her letter?

She slipped a piece of paper into the typewriter. There was no time like the present. But before she had begun Latham Elliot burst into the room again, his piercing black eyes impaling her. 'What does she say?' he demanded, snatching up the vital letter before she had time to cover it, his eyes flicking over the few closely written lines, hardening as he got to the end.

He flung it back in contempt. 'At least now I have a lead. Thanks for your help, Susi.'

Before she could say another word he had gone. She chased after him, catching him up in the yard outside the house. 'Latham, what are you doing? You can't go to Alison. You can't make her tell you where Carl is, I won't let you. I want to see him first. I'm sure he's sorry for what he did. Let me talk to him. I want to tell him about Mum and Dad. If you get to him before me you'll kill him, I know you will, and I'll never forgive you. I'll see you in hell!'

'You think he hasn't put me there?' he demanded bitterly, nostrils flaring, eyes hard and bright. 'It's no more than he deserves.'

'God, how I hate you!' Susi pounded her fists passionately against his chest. 'I've never met a man so cruel. How can you do this to me? It's inhuman!'

'If anyone's made me like this, it's that brother of yours. I've been waiting a long time to get my hands on him. I'm certainly not going to let him slip through my fingers now. But——' he paused and looked at her speculatively, 'I think I might let you do the dirty work. I really have no inclination to see Alison again—I might kill her too. You can go and see her, you can get Carl's address, you can have your talk—and then——'

'You'll swoop in to make your kill?' interjected Susi acidly. 'You don't really expect me to lead you to him?'

He shrugged expressively. 'If you want to see your brother it's the only way you'll be able to do it. There's no other way that you'll be able to get out of this house—I'll make sure of that.'

'You're despicable!' Anger flashed in her green eyes.

He smiled grimly. 'It's not the only name I've been called. What's your answer, Susi?'

'You know there can only be one,' she thrust, breathing hard, her breasts rising and falling, her heart slamming painfully against her rib cage. 'I want to see Carl.'

'Then we'll go and find Alison now,' he said with a finality that brooked no refusal.

'She might not be in. She wasn't there the day I went to see her. Perhaps she works?'

'Alison work?' he scoffed derisively. 'She's a lady of leisure. If she's not in then we wait.'

But Alison was at home. Latham sat in the car while Susi climbed the two flights of stairs to her flat, scorning the lift. Her heart banged like a sledgehammer as she pressed her finger on the bell push.

The girl who opened the door was much as Susi had expected—a smart, brittle woman with an over made-up face and a voluptuous figure. Her dyed blonde hair was shoulder-length, casually waved, her cornflower blue eyes sharp and enquiring.

Susi privately decided that Latham had had a narrow escape. Alison Cordell would never have made a farmer's wife. 'I'm Susi Kingswood,' she said, when the woman had looked at her for several long seconds without speaking.

'You wasted no time, I must say.' The woman registered surprise. 'I suppose you'd better come in.' She peered along the corridor as though expecting to see someone behind her. 'Is Latham Elliot with you?'

'He's in the car,' acknowledged Susi. 'I expect you know the reason he didn't come up?'

There was a sudden tightening of the other woman's features, a hardening of her eyes, but her voice when she spoke was carefully controlled. 'How is he? It must be well over two years since I've seen him.'

'Since the accident,' accused Susi bitterly, unable to help herself.

The finely pencilled brows rose. 'I see he has a champion in you. How touching! And it's clear he's told you about me.' She shrugged with assumed indifference.

'If you must know,' cried Susi angrily, 'I think it was a very cruel thing that you did.'

'Latham's big and strong enough to look after himself,' said Alison contemptuously. 'He was never short of female company before he met me, I'm quite sure he's never been short since.'

That's all you know, thought Susi. It wasn't the accident that had done the lasting damage, but this woman's treatment of him. Though why he had fallen in love with her in the first place, she would never know. So far as she could see Alison Cordell did not have one endearing characteristic.

'I suppose you're in love with him yourself?' asked Alison crudely. 'There's no accounting for taste, is there? Like them rough, do you? I can't say I'd like to tie myself to a man who's had his face torn open.'

'The scar isn't that bad,' cried Susi defensively. 'As

you'd have found out if you'd waited round long
enough.'

'I can't bear illness.' The woman's lips curled
distastefully. 'But enough about Latham. You want to
see Carl, I take it? You're wasting your time. He says he
doesn't know why you've come to Australia, but he
certainly doesn't want to see you.'

'I can't believe that Carl would say that,' said Susi. 'I
have something personal I want to tell him. Tell me
where he is, Alison, please. It's very important.'

'You don't fool me,' returned the other girl bitterly.
'I know why you want to find him. You're doing it for
Latham. He's put you up to this, hasn't he? You've
played right into his hands, coming out to visit your
brother, and now he's hoping you'll lead him to Carl.'

'That's not so,' protested Susi strongly, hating this
woman more with every minute that passed. 'I know how
Latham Elliot feels, believe me, and no way am I going to
reveal my brother's whereabouts. I love Carl. It's because
I love him that I'm here now. I must see him.'

'Why?' jeered the blonde. 'Why is it suddenly so
important?'

'That's my affair,' said Susi. 'It's private, between me
and Carl. Is he in Sydney? Can I go and see him now?'

'You don't think he'd be fool enough to hang around
here?' Alison Cordell's cold blue, carefully outlined,
eyes flashed disdainfully. 'As a matter of fact I haven't
seen him myself in over twelve months.'

'Meaning things didn't work out between you two
either?'

'It was never intended to be a permanent arrange-
ment,' announced Alison. 'We had an affair, and I
helped him when he ran away from Latham. But I like
my men rich. Carl was never able to keep me in the
manner to which I'm accustomed.'

One glance at her sumptuous apartment told Susi that. 'Yet you gave Latham up?'

'I like them rich *and* handsome,' said Alison nastily. 'I like other woman to look at me in envy, not pity, when I'm out with a man.'

How sorry Susi felt for Latham right at that moment! If Alison had spoken to him like this when he was in hospital it was no wonder he was bitter and disillusioned. No wonder he felt he had no right to ask any other woman to share his life! 'I haven't come here to discuss Latham,' she said coldly. 'I want to know where Carl is. I'm not going until you give me a satisfactory answer.'

Alison eyed her disdainfully. 'I'll write again and tell him you say it's important.'

'Why don't you give me his address and let me write?'

'Oh, no,' said the blonde woman quickly. 'I don't trust you. If Latham finds out and goes after Carl he would blame me. He could turn nasty.'

'And so just because you want to save your own pretty face you're not prepared to help?'

'I said I'd write,' said Alison tightly. 'And that's as much as I'm prepared to do.' She snatched open the door. 'Please go now, you'll be hearing from me as soon as I have word from Carl. Make sure Latham doesn't read the letter.'

There was nothing else Susi could do. She swallowed her disappointment and on leaden feet walked out of the apartment.

'Well?' said Latham, immediately she had lowered herself into his car.

'No luck,' she confessed sadly. 'Alison is afraid I'll give it to you. But she's going to write to him again and see what he says.'

'God!' he rasped savagely. 'You've mishandled the whole affair. I should have gone to see Alison myself.'

'It wouldn't have helped.' Susi looked at him apologetically. 'Alison's feelings towards you haven't changed.'

His lips firmed, a pulse quivering in the strong line of his jaw.

'I'm sorry,' said Susi. 'But if it's any consolation she's not seeing Carl either. I don't think the affair lasted long.'

'You think I still care?' he sneered. 'Carl did me a good turn. I never knew Alison was so shallow. She really had me fooled. I thought she loved me. I knew my money helped, but so far as I was concerned that didn't matter. But even that meant less to her than the horror of being tied to a man who was less than physically perfect.'

'She's stupid,' said Susi strongly. 'If she'd waited round long enough she'd have seen it wasn't so bad as she feared. In time she'd not have even noticed.'

'Don't start that again, for pity's sake,' thrust Latham angrily. 'You're as bad as Alison, except that she had the guts to tell me to my face what she thought. She didn't put on an act just because she felt sorry for me.'

'Sorry for you?' Susi's eyes widened. 'I don't feel sorry for you, Latham. You feel sorry for yourself, that's the top and bottom of your trouble.'

He refused to answer, putting the car into drive and shooting off at an alarming rate into the dense traffic.

Neither of them spoke on the journey back to Kalabara. It was a long and uncomfortable ride and Susi was glad when it was over. The whole morning had been a waste of time. She had achieved nothing. She could have written to Alison and done as much.

The men had already had their lunch. Jake grumbled goodnaturedly, 'They don't like my cooking. You've spoilt them. I've received nothing but insults.'

She smiled briefly. 'I'm sorry. I had a letter from Alison this morning and I've been to see her.'

'With Latham?' His brows shot up. 'Why did you tell him?'

'I had no choice,' she confessed. 'He saw the letter and recognised her writing. I didn't know that they were once thinking of getting married. I didn't even know they knew each other. I wish you'd told me.'

'I didn't think it necessary.' He looked worried. 'I didn't think he'd find out you'd been to see her. I really have put my foot in it, haven't I? I assume he's found out that it was me who gave you her address?'

'I'm afraid so,' she admitted ruefully. 'But if it means I find Carl then it will be all thanks to you.'

'Not if Latham gets to him first,' said Jake, his brow creased in anguish.

'I'll see that he doesn't. It's my brother, don't forget. I can be tough if I want to be. I shall make sure Latham doesn't find Carl before I do.'

Jake shook his head sadly. 'You be careful, girl. I've known Latham a long time, and he has a perfectly reasonable hatred for your brother. No man takes lightly to being assaulted like he was. He'll stop at nothing to get his own back.'

'I'm well aware of that,' said Susi. 'It's going to be quite a game, but I have every confidence that I'll succeed.'

'You're some girl, Susi. I wish you luck. I also wish I'd kept my big mouth shut.' Jake looked glum.

Susi did not feel like working in Latham's study that afternoon. She went for a swim instead, finding relief in the crystal-clear water, lying afterwards in the sun, refusing to let her mind dwell on her immediate problems. She was doing only what she had to do, what any self-respecting girl would do.

When a shadow fell over her she knew immediately who it was. 'What do you want?' she asked without opening her eyes.

'I want to know what you're doing here.'

'Isn't it obvious?' She squinted through her lashes, noting surprisingly that he had his trunks on too. The sun gilded his copper chest, highlighting the scars, making Susi turn her head away. How could her brother have done this to him?

She began to understand why Latham hated Carl so much, why he swore that he would kill him if he caught up with him again. It was not often that she saw Latham's chest, but when she did it reminded her much more clearly of what her brother had done.

And Latham saw them every day! He had a constant and permanent reminder of Carl's attack. There was no chance that he would ever be able to forget it. They would be with him for the rest of his life.

'You should be working!' The coldness in his voice made her shiver despite the heat of the sun.

'It's too hot,' she protested. 'I'll do your typing this evening instead.'

'You mean you're too idle. It's getting too much for you, is that it? At last you're beginning to realise that working for me isn't all wine and roses.'

Susi glanced at him sharply, haughtily, her green eyes flashing with anger. 'I never thought it would be that, but I don't see why I shouldn't enjoy the sun sometimes.'

'Not when there's work to be done,' he growled.

'And if you have your way you'll see that there's something to keep me occupied for twenty-four hours of the day.' She pushed herself to her feet, wishing she had a few more inches so that she did not have to tilt back her head to look him in the eye.

The jet black depths were unfathomable, boring into her, filling her with unexpected excitement. 'You're coming the mighty I am, is that it?' she demanded. 'As a matter of fact I've finished my swim. I was going indoors in a few moments anyway.'

This was not strictly true because she had intended remaining out here until it was time to cook their evening meal, but she had to get back at him some way. She sauntered in the direction of the house and the next moment heard a splash as Latham dived expertly into the water.

She turned and watched as his powerful arms cleaved the water. Length upon length he did, ceaselessly, tirelessly. Susi guessed it was his way of working off his insufferably bad mood. She felt deeply for him and wished there was something she could do.

For the next few days Latham worked Susi hard. She did not stop from the time she got up until she went to bed, and by then she was so completely worn out that she fell asleep the moment her head touched the pillow.

She felt quite sure that had he been doing the office work himself he would not have found so much to do. The files did not really need sorting out, or those figures copied into a new ledger. Trying to cook the meals and keep the house clean in between, not to mention the washing and ironing, was draining her of every ounce of energy.

Even Jake remarked on how peaky she was looking. 'You're doing too much,' he grumbled. 'You shouldn't let Latham work you like that. You surprise me. I thought you'd stick up to him. You've had no free time at all this last week.'

'It's since I went to see Alison,' admitted Susi ruefully. 'I think it raked up memories for Latham and he's venting his temper on me. But I'm not going to give him the pleasure of hearing me complain—that's not my way at all. If necessary I'll work till I drop.'

Jake shook his head, compressing his lips. 'You're a fool, Susi, and no mistake. Do you want me to have a word with him?'

'No!' she said quickly, strongly. 'He'll think I've been complaining.'

And then at long last came the awaited letter from Alison. As on the previous occasion Latham had separated it from the rest of the mail, and held it out to her as she entered the office after breakfast.

Although she would have preferred to read it in private she knew that Latham was quite capable of following her, so she slit open the envelope there and then, turning her back to read the brief message.

> *Carl refuses to see you. He insists you go back to England. Don't try to contact him again.*
> *Alison Cordell*

Susi felt like bursting into tears. Instead she swung round angrily and shoved the piece of paper under Latham's nose, watching him tensely as he read the couple of lines.

There was no hint of emotion on his face, nothing to give away what he was thinking. It was probably no more or no less than he had expected.

'So that's that,' she said flatly. 'There's nothing else I can do. I'd hire a private detective if I could afford one, but it's out of the question. I suppose I'll have to tell him about Mum and Dad in a letter and ask Alison to forward it. It won't be the same, but he has a right to know.'

Latham rose and walked round the desk, standing at her side. 'You're giving up? Where's that fighting spirit I so much admired?'

She shrugged, ignoring the hammering of her heart. It always throbbed when he came this close. It was a purely physical thing that she was unable to do anything about. It had never done it with any other man and she wished with all her heart it did not happen with Latham.

'I don't have your kind of money,' she said. 'I'm surprised you haven't done so, though, considering how strongly you feel about him.'

'And end up in jail myself for murder?' he said savagely. 'No, thanks, Susi. I'll bide my time. Our paths will cross again one day. Meanwhile let him suffer. He knows I won't forget. He must have led one hell of a life these last two years, wondering when I'm going to turn up. He's suffering, believe me. He'll probably go on suffering for the rest of his life, if he doesn't do something else stupid. Either way he'll get what's coming to him.'

The lines of strain had never been more deeply etched. His whole body was as tense as a bowstring, and Susi blamed herself. If she hadn't come looking for Carl, brought the whole sorry thing out into the open once again, Latham would not be torturing himself like this.

But she was stupid letting it bother her, when he deserved it. For three weeks now she had worked her fingers to the bone, scrubbing and polishing, cooking and typing, all without a penny's reward, all because Latham Elliot had decided she should be the one to pay off Carl's debts.

'You do realise it's my brother you're talking about,' she said crossly, more angry with herself for letting

Latham affect her than anything else. She really ought to get away from here as soon as possible. He was getting beneath her skin in a way she had let no other man. He was creeping under the defensive wall she had built so carefully around herself.

'It's something I'm never likely to forget,' he said grimly.

'In that case, I may as well go back to England. I refuse to remain here and listen to you running him down!'

He remained unperturbed. 'I thought you came out on a one-way ticket?'

'So what?'

'Then how will you get back?'

She swallowed hard. 'I—I'll get a proper job somewhere and save up. I refuse to spend the rest of my life working for nothing—you can't make me!'

'I thought you liked it here?' His brows rose mockingly, his black eyes never leaving her face. 'You made a point once of telling me that the work was no hardship.'

'And you pointed out that you would go on adding to my workload until I found it too much to bear,' she returned crossly. 'These last few days I haven't had a minute to call my own.'

'You're admitting it's too much?' There was an odd gleam in those dark eyes.

Susi felt suddenly very tired. The letter from Alison had been the last straw. There was no point in letting Latham put on her any longer. 'That's right,' she admitted bitterly.

'I never thought I'd hear you say it.' He looked delighted.

Susi felt like hitting him. 'If I thought there was any chance of me seeing Carl I never would have. I would have gone on until I'd found him. I was using you just as much as you were using me. Don't think I'm frightened of you, because I'm not. I'm going now, and there's no way that you can stop me!'

Surprisingly he smiled. 'I'm glad your fighting spirit's come back, that Carl's refusal to see you hasn't broken it. It would have been a pity. You're one hell of a woman, Susi, do you know that?'

He reached out and took her shoulders, and this time there was no bruising aggression. His hands were firm yet gentle, his black eyes unusually soft. 'I have a proposition to put to you.'

Susi's lashes flicked upwards, framing her lovely eyes. 'It has to be devious. I'm not sure that I want to hear it.'

Latham shook his head as if unable to understand her startled reaction. 'It's quite straightforward, I assure you. You're right, Susi, I have no power to keep you. You're free to go any time you want. But you're doing such a good job I'd be reluctant to let you go.'

'If you think I'm going to slave here out of the goodness of my heart you're mistaken!' she blazed.

'I was suggesting,' he returned levelly, 'that I take you on as a regular member of my staff. I would pay you a good salary. My only stipulation would be that you stay for at least twelve months, that you wouldn't skip off back to England once you'd saved enough money.' His black eyes had never been more powerful. 'What do you say, Susi? Is it a deal?'

Susi was completely bewildered by this sudden turn of events. 'I don't know. I'd like time to think.'

'How long?' he asked quickly, and the pressure of his fingers increased. 'A few hours? Is that enough?'

She shook her head, feeling suddenly limp. 'Till tomorrow. I'll tell you in the morning. I'd like to sleep on it.'

'Till tomorrow, then,' he said easily. 'And I think I can promise that if you say yes you won't regret it.'

Susi was not so sure. Latham was an extremely sexually attractive man. She already felt strongly drawn towards him; lord knows how she would feel in twelve months. She was not sure that she would be able to handle it. Not if Latham's attitude towards her and women in general did not change.

The atmosphere would be unbearable if, every time she rejected his advances, he thought it was because she found him repulsive. He could not seem to accept the fact that she simply did not want him to kiss her, that even if he had been scarless it would have made no difference. The truth was she was frightened of her own feelings!

It must have crushed his ego completely when Alison let him down, made him think that he was only half a man, and in Latham's eyes that made him no man at all.

She twisted away from his grasp and he let her go easily. Never had she been more aware of him than she was at this moment. Her pulses throbbed with a sensuality that sent spirals of flame licking through her limbs. Her heart raced fit to burst. The blood pounded in her head and she knew that her answer was going to be yes.

'How about that trip to the beach I promised you?' suggested Latham surprisingly.

Susi shot him a wide-eyed startled glance. This was blackmail in the extreme. Every hour spent in his company, especially when he was in this particularly friendly mood, was going to be hard. 'I don't know,' she prevaricated. 'I'm not sure it would be a good idea.'

'It would help drive your blues away,' he said gently. 'I know you're upset over your brother's refusal to see you, and contrary to what you might think, I do understand how you feel—I'm not that coldhearted. It would do us both good. We'll pack some food and have a barbecue. You'll enjoy it, I promise.'

Susi smiled weakly. 'You win! I must admit I don't think I'd be able to concentrate on your typing.'

'Come along, then.' He looked boyish all of a sudden, grinning widely, eyes sparkling. 'What are we waiting for?'

They went through into the kitchen and he packed a cold box with crushed ice before placing in a bottle of wine, plus steaks and salad. He piled in far too much food, thought Susi, as he added two generous portions of the apple pie she had cooked for the men's lunch.

At last he pronounced himself satisfied. 'Now we will get changed. Put on your bikini—and something to cover yourself up with. You've not yet acquired sufficient tan to stay out in the sun too long.'

Which is your fault, thought Susi, but prudently kept her thoughts to herself. She selected a jade green bikini with its own matching wrapover mini-dress. On her head she sat a straw hat that she had bought in Sydney the day they went shopping, and pushed her feet into a pair of thongs, as Latham had told her they were called, laughing when she referred to them as flip-flops. He had made her buy them, saying that absolutely everyone wore thongs whether they were out for a picnic or simply walking about the shops. His were leather, her own rubber—all she could afford.

She added a couple of large towels to her bag and then went outside to find Latham already waiting in his car. It was not the big flash limousine but a low sports car with an open top. Susi pulled a wry face as she looked at it and took off her hat.

There was something exhilarating about driving

through the Australian countryside with Latham in the silver car, her hair streaming out behind her in a thick dark mane. She laughed with sheer enjoyment.

Latham glanced obliquely across. 'It's good to see you happy. You've been far too serious lately.'

'And whose fault is that?' she demanded, but was not cross.

He inclined his head. 'Guilty,' he said with laughter in his voice. 'But things will change now you're working for me proper.'

'I haven't said yet that I'm prepared to do it.' Susi shot him an accusing glare.

'Oh, no, I'd forgotten. I was taking it for granted. But you will, I'm sure.'

He turned off the main road and followed a winding track. Conversation was forgotten as Susi looked about her with interest. The thick bush that she had only seen in the distance spread out on all sides. Latham pointed out tree trunks blackened by tongues of flame following a bushfire. Branches twisted and distorted by the heat of the flames, leaning drunkenly against one another. He indicated an acacia with its open seedpods. 'Burst open by the fire,' he explained. 'It's the way they propagate.'

The sight of so much desolation saddened Susi. She had seen television newsreels about bushfires in Australia, always worrying whether Carl was safe. It was a terrible, terrible thing—homes going up in flame, possessions of a lifetime lost in seconds. Yet already the bush was springing back to life, fresh growth pushing its way through the blackened vegetation.

Gradually the bush grew more dense and Latham stopped the car. They got out, listening to the call of the birds, animals shuffling in the undergrowth.

Latham appeared to be looking for something. He

stood still and silent for several long minutes, finally putting his hand on her arm, then a finger to his lips, pointing to a clearing not many yards away.

She saw them clearly—kangaroos; four of them. They looked like a family. There were two tall ones and two smaller ones. They were standing up straight looking in their direction, their two little forepaws hanging down, their heads up and slightly back, balancing on their tails.

'They always pose like that when they're alarmed,' whispered Latham. 'One false move and they'll be gone. It must be our lucky day.'

'They're beautiful,' said Susi in a hushed voice. 'I never realised they were so big.'

'Bucks can grow to a height of seven feet,' Latham told her, 'the does about five, and they can travel at tremendous speed. When I was a lad I once went out on a hunt with a farmer who was troubled by roos on his land—they can be a pest, you know. I remember watching the speedo. We averaged about thirty-three miles an hour and each of their hops must have been twenty-five feet.

'Actually the doe is quicker, because she's much lighter. Have you ever heard the term, "Blue flyer"? It's a maiden doe about eighteen months old, and some have been clocked at nearly forty miles an hour. They can run for five miles at full speed without stopping, their hops covering as much as thirty feet. At half speed they can travel twenty miles.'

'That's incredible,' said Susi loudly—too loudly. Her voice carried to the poised animals and with one movement of their strong back legs they leapt away and were swallowed up in the bush.

'Oh, I'm sorry,' she said immediately.

Latham grinned ruefully. 'I expected it. Don't blame yourself.'

'But they were so cute. Perhaps they'll come back?'

'I doubt it,' he said. 'They'll be far away by now.'

'How old do you reckon the young ones were?'

He shrugged. 'It takes them four years to become adult, so they might be about two. They actually use their mother's pouch as transport until they're too big to fit in—usually at about nine months.'

'I saw a documentary on television once,' said Susi. 'It showed how the embryo leaves the womb after only a few weeks' gestation. It looked like a grub.'

'That's right,' acceded Latham. 'They're born undeveloped and are only about half an inch long. They crawl through their mother's fur and into the pouch. There they attach themselves to one of her teats. They actually clamp their mouth on so firmly that they can't be pulled away without rupturing their lips.'

Susi found this truly amazing. 'How on earth do they manage to suck milk if they're so immature?'

He smiled. 'It's forced into the embryo's throat by a natural pumping action in the mother's breast.'

'Isn't nature wonderful?' she breathed. 'Do the kangaroos have more than one baby at a time?'

Latham nodded. 'Sometimes they give birth again before the young joey is ready to leave the pouch, in which case the new baby attaches itself to another of the mother's teats. Or, for instance, if anything happens to the embryo before it reaches its mother's pouch then a new one will emerge and take its place.'

'I'm glad you told me all this,' said Susi. 'It's fascinating. Oh, I do love Australia!'

Up above magpie-larks carolled, their liquid music filling the air, putting their English brothers to shame. Occasionally she caught flashes of colour as rosellas and parrots flitted through the thick foliage.

There were wild flowers such as she had never seen

before—some that looked like red and yellow bottle-brushes, which Latham told her were called banksia, often attended by honeyeaters—birds with long beaks. There were tiny pink wax-like, star-shaped flowers, that looked impossibly delicate, and various heaths spread out in all directions.

It was a veritable paradise of sights and colours and scents, and Susi was sorry when Latham suggested they carry on.

A few minutes later the road dipped suddenly and they wound downhill until they ended right on a deserted beach. The surf pounded the sugary sand, white-crested waves rolling in long dramatic lines.

'We must try body-surfing one day,' said Latham when he saw her watching the curling foam. 'Now, we're going to relax and enjoy ourselves.'

It was not long before he had everything out of the car heaped on the beach. 'It's a bit early to eat, don't you think?' he said.

'We must swim!' exclaimed Susi, her eyes shining. 'The water's so inviting.' It was the most vivid blue-green she had ever seen, reflecting the colour of the cloudless sky, shimmering in the silver rays of the sun.

Behind them sandstone cliffs rose majestically, skirted by boulders and rocks which she thought it would be nice to go climbing afterwards, changing her mind immediately she saw a lizard sunning itself on the nearest one.

She kicked off her thongs, slipped off her dress, and ran forward into the creaming surf. It was like silk on her skin, cool and invigorating, and she had been swimming for several minutes before she realised that Latham had not joined her.

Instead he stood watching, strong legs apart, arms akimbo, a perfect specimen of prime manhood, of masculine sexuality. 'Aren't you coming in?' she called, wondering whether she would ever be able to look at him without her heartbeats quickening. 'Or are you going to stand there all day?'

'I'm admiring your movements.' His voice was only just audible above the pounding waves.

Susi felt inordinately pleased and dived back beneath the waves, surfacing a few seconds later to find Latham at her side. They swam for a few minutes before deciding there was no sense in tiring themselves out. A day of leisure, Latham had said.

Spreading out her towel, she threw herself down. This was surely the most peaceful spot in the world. She closed her eyes, feeling the heat of the sun dry her in seconds.

It came as a sudden shock when she felt Latham begin to smooth sun cream into her legs. She shot up, but he pushed her back peremptorily, grinning broadly.

'I can do it myself,' she protested, laughter in her voice, reluctant to admit, even to herself, that she liked the feel of his hand on her skin. There was something erotic about the way he was doing it, the slow movements causing the blood to race in her veins.

'It's my pleasure,' he demurred. 'Surely you're not going to deprive me?' His black eyes had never been more gentle, giving Susi the impression that he was being nice to her because he wanted her to continue working at the stud.

But once she was his official employee, what then? Would he be as hard a taskmaster as he had ever been? Would he work her until she was ready to drop? She hated to admit this, but she did not trust Latham Elliot one inch.

All the same she could not ignore the sensations that ran through her, and she knew that any minute his hands would move up to her stomach and midriff, her arms and shoulders, and the exposed area of her breasts.

Her stomach tightened at the thought of him performing so intimate a task. Already her heart clamoured loud enough to be heard. It would be a total giveaway when he rested his hand on it.

She sat up again and held out her hand for the bottle. 'I really would prefer to do it myself. Give it to me.'

He drew in his breath in a swift angry jerk, a pulse beating suddenly and fiercely in his jaw, his eyes hard, hiding his pain at her rejection.

Susi could have kicked herself. Always she made him feel bad. But there was nothing she could do now. If she tried to apologise, if she tried to explain, he would think they were excuses. The best thing she could do was to act as though nothing was the matter.

She poured cream into her palm and applied it to all the parts that she could reach, then looked at Latham, who was lying on his stomach, his head turned away from her. 'You could do my back,' she suggested tentatively.

Slowly he rolled over and looked at her. There was tight anger on his face. 'It's no use being sorry now, no use trying to pretend. I know exactly how you feel. You don't want to hurt me, I know that, but your reactions are totally involuntary, and they tell me more than anything else that you dislike me touching you.'

'It's not true,' protested Susi. 'It doesn't bother me at—well, not in the way you think.'

He snarled, 'There's only one reason why a woman doesn't like a man to touch her, and that's because she finds him repulsive, so don't try and come up with excuses, because they won't wash. I've had enough experience over the last two years to be able to judge reactions for myself.'

'Then you should know that I'm telling you the truth!'

He sat up, withering her with one glance from those hard eyes. 'You tell me why. Spell it out. Let's have it. Go on—I'm waiting.'

Susi avoided looking at him, wondering exactly how to put into words, without making a fool of herself, that she felt a physical attraction—a very strong physical attraction. One that could not be denied. She had tried once before and he had not believed her. What chance was there that he would now? He was convinced no one would ever be charmed by him again. He felt that he had nothing to offer, and no one would ever change his mind about that.

Admittedly he had relaxed somewhat in his attitude towards her. He no longer seemed so self-conscious about his scars—until she reminded him of them by her own thoughtless actions!

'You see,' he said loudly and angrily, 'there's nothing you can say.'

'It's difficult to put it into words,' said Susi, 'but I don't find you offensive, I really don't, and I would like you to do my back.' She held out the bottle and mentally crossed her fingers that he would oblige. It would at least be a step in the right direction.

After what seemed an age Latham took the bottle, but whereas before his actions had been sensual, stroking her limbs as though he enjoyed what he was doing, now he attended to the matter briskly, with an air of clinical detachment. It took him no more than a few seconds to smooth in the lotion and then the bottle was thrust back with an aggression that could not be ignored.

'Why do I always rub you up the wrong way?' asked Susi sadly. 'I don't mean to. Life's too short to be spent arguing.'

'In that case,' he crisped, 'you should learn to think before you speak. It's not easy to live with my disfigurement.'

Susi did not want to spoil this day any more. He had done his best to atone for the disappointment she felt on receipt of Alison's letter, and now inadvertently she had ruined it. 'I'll try,' she said, and smiled weakly, holding out her hand in a gesture of friendship.

After a long hesitation, when she thought he was going to ignore her, he took her hand. But he held it for no more than a second, jumping up and saying briskly, 'Time for the barbecue.'

It did not take him long to set up the portable barbecue and in no time at all the coals were hot enough to cook the steaks. Susi split open the crusty loaf and spread it thickly with butter, sorting out the salad, sampling the tempting onion dip on the end of a piece of celery while waiting for the meat. She was incredibly hungry.

When all was finally ready Latham had got over his ill-humour and they talked the whole way through the meal. She discovered that his parents had died in a bushfire when he was only twelve and that he had more or less brought himself up.

He had travelled the whole of the continent and had actually lived with the aboriginals for a while in Arnhem Land, which, he explained, was the north-eastern tip of the so called Northern Territory.

'Some of my happiest memories are with the aboriginals,' he admitted. 'They have some strange ideas, admittedly, but I found them a completely fascinating race.'

'Has the name of your farm anything to do with them?' asked Susi. 'It's a lovely name. I wondered what it meant.'

'Kalabara? Yes, it's a mythical red kangaroo about which all sorts of tales have been woven. Perhaps I'll tell you about them one day.'

He was taking it for granted that she would stay, thought Susi, but she did not care because she had more or less made up her mind anyway.

After they had finished eating they lay down again. Susi felt drowsy but did not realise that she had fallen asleep until she suddenly came to and found her head on Latham's chest. When she tried to move she discovered his arm across her and glancing at him saw that he was asleep too.

She wondered how they had managed to get into this position, whether she had snuggled up against Latham as she slept, or whether he had instigated it. Not that it mattered. She was here and there was nothing she could do about it without waking him.

She took the opportunity to study his face. It was the first time she had done so without him feeling that she was staring at his scar. There was no aggression now, in fact a smile curved his sensuous lips, making her wonder what thoughts were going through his mind. Even the lines that the last two years had created were softened and practically invisible. There was a vulnerability about him that made her breath catch in her throat.

On the outside he was hard, but underneath he was afraid of people looking at him. He hated her brother for what he had done, he hated Alison for the way she had treated him. In fact he hated the whole world. Only with herself was he beginning to unbend. She did not need to be told that she was the first woman who had been near him since the accident.

There was no way, though, that she could ignore his scars, particularly the one on his face. It drew her eyes time and time again. It was like a jagged question mark, and without realising what she was doing Susi ran her fingers lightly over the cicatrice, feeling the uneven shape of the skin, but experiencing no revulsion.

If only it had been some other man who had done this to him! He might have allowed himself to get closer to her. As things stood she was a permanent reminder. He would never let her into his private life.

He probably thought there was still a chance that she and Carl would get together, that one day her brother would contact her. He was probably using her as bait!

This sudden thought shocked her. Why hadn't she thought of it before? It must be the reason he had asked her to stay. But by so doing she could lead Carl into danger, and this was not what she wanted at all. He might be a criminal, a potential killer even, but he was her brother, and that meant more to her than anything else. It was bad enough losing her parents, she did not want to lose Carl too. Even though there was no contact at the moment he was at least family, and she clung to that like she had clung to nothing in her life.

Susi was unaware that all the time these thoughts flitted through her head her hand still rested on Latham's face. When suddenly his fingers shot round her wrist, dragging her hand away, she wondered what had hit her.

'What are you doing?' he demanded, his face as white as a corpse. 'Touch me again like that and I'll bloody well kill you as well as that brother of yours!'

CHAPTER FIVE

Susi jumped as though she had been shot, jerking backwards, her eyes wide and apprehensive. 'I wasn't hurting you, was I?' Her breasts rose and fell as her breathing deepened, her heart hammered against her breast bone.

'Of course you weren't damn well hurting,' he grated, 'but I'm not a freak in a circus. I can do without you examining my wounds. Attracted despite yourself were you?' His lips curled savagely. 'Wanted to see if they felt as repulsive as they look, is that it?'

Susi quivered, sitting back on her heels. 'I don't feel horrified.' Her eyes were soft and compassionate and she wanted to take him into her arms, assure him that the scars made no difference to him as a man, that he was vitally attractive and no woman in her right mind would ever think otherwise.

'Then I don't want your pity either,' he snapped. 'That would be even worse. It's what I got from Jake and some of the others to start with, but now they ignore it—and I advise you to do the same if you want a happy working relationship.'

'I don't feel sorry for you,' said Susi quietly. 'You've got one hell of a chip on your shoulder, and until you get rid of it you'll never relax with a woman again. You seem to think that all she's looking at, that all she ever thinks about, is your scars. Well, I can tell you that that's not true. They're noticeable, admittedly, but easy to forget. With a personality like yours, Latham, it wouldn't matter if you were the ugliest man in the

105

world, you've got all and more than any man could ask for. If it bothers you that much why don't you grow a beard—or even have plastic surgery?'

The anger in his eyes had never been more intense. 'I didn't ask for your opinion, nor do I want it. What I do with my face is my own affair. Thanks for ruining the day, Susi. I thought I was doing you a favour. I should have known better.' He pushed himself savagely to his feet and began loading the barbecue gear back into his car.

Once it was carefully stowed away he tugged on his black cords and white tee-shirt, turning at length to Susi. 'Are you ready? If not, I'll leave you here, and don't think I'll lose any sleep over it.'

She had stood and watched, frozen into immobility, wanting to help, but unable to force her limbs to move. Suddenly she became conscious that she was shivering and she pulled on the dress which Latham had left lying on the sand as though it were vermin.

Stiffly she walked to the car, sliding into it and snapping the seat-belt, keeping as far away from Latham as she could. The very first time she had met him she had decided he was vitriolic. He had not changed. Never was any man so damning in his treatment. His words seared through her like a knife, making her wince at each slice of the blade.

As the little car climbed the winding road Susi could not help wondering what sort of a man Latham Elliot would become if he continued torturing himself. She guessed she was the first person to have spoken to him so bluntly, but it had done no good. In fact it had probably done more harm. He resented her looking at him, and had been absolutely infuriated when she touched him. She had never known a man so sensitive about his appearance—and blamed it all on Alison.

If the woman had hung around long enough she would have discovered the scars were nowhere near as bad as she had feared. If she had remained Latham would have accepted his disfigurement and not made such an issue of it.

Alison was the most callous, cold-hearted person she had ever come across. By her own thoughtless actions she had ruined Latham's life, and had no remorse at all about doing so. He can look after himself, she had said.

But it had played on Latham's mind, affecting him far more deeply than anyone would guess. Unreasonably so, in Susi's opinion, but there was nothing that could be done about that. His feeling of inferiority had grown out of all proportion to the actual scars, but he would listen to no one. So far as he was concerned it had put a stop to his love life. There was nothing left for him except running his stud farm in this out-of-the-way place.

The atmosphere between them was electric. She would not have been surprised to see sparks flying from one to the other. Although neither spoke, the tension that filled the car, despite its open roof, was such as she had never experienced in her life, nor would she like to go through it again.

Although the journey was short it seemed to last a lifetime. Her whole body responded to Latham. She wanted more than anything to reassure him that he was being over-sensitive about the whole affair, but she knew it was useless. He would listen to no one, especially not her, the sister of the man who had been his downfall.

She wondered whether she ought to leave, whether her assumption was correct and he was using her to get to Carl. He would never be satisfied until he came face to face with him again, until justice had been done, whether at his own hands, or through the hands of the law.

She found herself torn two ways. Part of her wanted to protect Carl, but the only way to do that was to go back to England.

On the other hand she was dangerously near to falling in love with this man. There was something about him that attracted her as irresistibly as metal to a magnet, and she knew that if she went away she would regret it for the rest of her life.

He was a man to surpass all men, proud, arrogant, undeniably aggressively masculine. She wished she had met him before the accident, seen exactly what kind of person he was prior to having his ego shattered. He must have been some man!

She had no doubt that he would eventually get over it, but it would be a long time. Two years had made no impression. He was so hard and embittered it looked as though he might go on this way for the rest of his life. She did not like to think so, no man should let a thing like this bother him indefinitely, but he was certainly not helping himself.

She wished she could help. More than anything in the world she would like to give of herself to Latham, reassure him that he was carrying his cross for nothing. Convince him that if he allowed himself to forget he could lead a much fuller life, a more rewarding life, a more enjoyable life. They were futile thoughts. He would never let her get that close.

She was glad when they were home, and she went straight to her room, stripping off her clothes and showering the salt water of the ocean from her skin. She dressed in a soft ivory cotton skirt and blouse, trimmed with broderie anglaise, and was pleased to see how her tan was deepening. She looked a picture of health, only her eyes were sad, and there was nothing she could do about that.

When she went through to the kitchen wondering what to do about their evening meal, knowing that the thought of food choked her, doubting whether Latham would want anything either, she met Jake. He gave her one of his familiar gap-toothed smiles. 'I've just been talking to the boss. He said he won't be wanting dinner this evening. It must have been some picnic you had!'

Susi attempted to return his smile, but it was a weak effort, although she knew she ought to do her best for Latham's sake. Jake had no idea that they had argued. He probably thought they had had a cosy few hours. There was certainly a twinkle in his pale blue eyes. She wondered exactly what Latham had told him.

'That's right,' she said, 'and I'm not hungry either.'

'In that case,' he grinned, 'I'll make myself a sandwich. No point in you putting yourself out for me. I'm glad you enjoyed your day—you deserve it. Latham tells me that you're gonna stay with us for a while, that he's taking you on his books proper. Is that a fact?'

Susi could not hide her surprise. 'I've not yet given him my answer.'

'He must be sure,' said Jake. 'Worked on you today, did he?'

'You could say that,' smiled Susi, but not in the way Jake was thinking. She looked around the kitchen which, considering Jake had had to do the lunches, was clean and tidy. 'If there's nothing to be done I may as well go back to my room.'

'How'd you like to take a walk round the stud?' he asked. 'You've not seen the horses yet. How long is it you've been here, three weeks?' Shame on you, girl, don't you like them? We have some real beauties.'

'I don't mind horses,' she admitted, 'but it's time I've been short of. However, I'd love to come now.'

But when they were out in the yard Susi wished she had not been so eager. Latham was saddling one of the horses. He looked surprised to see her with Jake, a thick frown blackening his brow. 'Were you looking for me?'

Jake answered for her. 'I was showing Susi around. Seems you missed out on that. If she's to be a regular employee I think she ought to see.'

Latham looked at Susi coldly. 'Is that what you want?'

She shrugged, glancing awkwardly up at him, wishing Jake had kept his mouth shut. 'I must admit I've been curious, but you've always said I was to keep away from the men, so I haven't bothered.'

A muscle jerked in his jaw, the skin tightened over his hard-boned face. 'Since you're here you may as well come for a ride. You can ride?'

It was an offer that would have delighted Susi had the circumstances been different. As they were, with Latham in this unbearable black mood, she had no desire to spend any time at all with him. 'No, thanks, I'm not dressed for riding.'

'I can wait.'

She could not believe that he wanted her to join him, so she shook her head vigorously, her auburn hair swirling about her pretty round face. She teased back the strands, then shielded her eyes from the glare of the sun. 'The answer's still no.'

'You mean it's because you don't want to go out with me?' The loaded question was shot at her strongly.

'If that's the way you care to interpret it,' she said. 'It's not what I'm saying.' In fact she would have liked to go out with him more than anything else.

He wore a pair of khaki jodhpurs that clung to every

muscle and sinew of his legs, accentuating the powerful thighs and firm calves. A thin white shirt moulded itself to his hard-muscled chest, and there was no denying his physical perfection. Sensual in the extreme.

They eyed each other for several seconds, Latham's black eyes penetrating her soul until she felt he was taking possession of her. Her stomach churned, her breathing became erratic. If he could affect her like this when he was angry with her, then what would happen if he really went out of his way to be nice? It was a mind-shattering thought, and one that she quickly squashed.

He fastened the final buckle and with swift angry movements swung himself into the saddle. He did not look at her again as he rode out of the yard. Susi regretted her decision immediately and wished she had gone with him. Maybe he was sorry for his outburst at the beach and wished to make amends? If that was the case she had done a good job of ruining that too. In fact she seemed to be making a pretty good job of spoiling everything.

With a rueful smile she turned back to Jake. 'I think I've seen enough. I have a book in my room. I'll lie down and read for a while. It's been a tiring day.'

He looked at her knowingly. 'If that's what you want—but you're a fool. Latham's a splendid guy. You should accept his offers of friendship. It's not very often he hands them out.'

Susi said nothing. All Jake saw was the chance of a ride, the picnic earlier. He really thought Latham was getting over his problem, and now blamed her for rejecting his peace offering.

'I have my reasons,' she said quietly. 'But they're none I'd care to discuss. I'm sorry, I don't mean to offend, but that's the way it is.'

Jake nodded as though he understood, but she knew

he did not. No one could possibly understand her predicament. 'I take it,' he said, 'that you'll be doing breakfast in the morning?'

She had to smile at that. Jake never let her forget that the men did not like his cooking, even though he himself did not mind doing it. She nodded, 'I'll be doing it,' and walked back into the house.

She did not go outside again that day and found difficulty in sleeping later. The cicadas were more insistent than ever. She had never heard a noise quite like it and was convinced that if they kept it up she would be awake for the whole night.

Eventually she did drop off, waking just before the sun rose to hear the peculiar laughter of the kookaburra. She had read about these birds, but it was the first time she had heard one. At first the harsh but well cadenced chuckle startled her, then she realised what it was and listened to the sound which began like harsh laughter and ended up with all sorts of peculiar garbled sounds.

And then the other birds joined in, ear-splitting shrieks, soft cooing, like nothing she had ever heard in England. It was as though all the birds in the world had congregated outside her window. It really was a lovely way to greet the morning.

But she must not forget that she had to give Latham her answer. He had taken it for granted that she would stay, even going so far as to tell Jake—which annoyed her. And she was still not sure! She had a feeling that she would regret it if she did agree, and twelve months was a long time if you were unhappy.

To her surprise she had a reprieve. Latham did not turn up for breakfast, and Susi asked Jake where he was.

'He went out early on Warrior,' he said. 'It's unusual

for him not to say where he's going if he's going to be out this long, on the other hand there's no reason why he should.'

'So he won't be back for breakfast?' Susi wondered whether she had anything to do with it, whether he was still angry because she had had the temerity to touch his facial scar. She had thought he was going to explode. He had been like a man demented, frightening her by his irrational behaviour.

Jake shook his head. 'Expect him when you see him, that's what he said.'

Susi went through to the office, but could not get Latham out of her mind. As time passed she began to wonder whether he had had an accident, whether he was lying unconscious somewhere. The more she thought about this the more worried she became, and in the end she could stand the uncertainty no longer.

She went and found Jake, explaining that she would like to go and look for Latham. 'Can I take one of the horses?'

'Some good that would do,' grumbled Jake good-naturedly. 'He'll be back soon, never fear. He won't have come to any harm.'

With that she had to be content, but found it difficult to concentrate on her typing. When she had made several mistakes she gave it up as a bad job and spent her time looking out of the window.

The fields were parched and empty, thirsty for rain, the sky a searing blue; even the birds were silent at this moment. Susi would never have believed that she could feel so unsettled by Latham's absence. It was nothing to do with her. There was no reason at all why she should be concerned.

Except that Latham got to her like no other man ever had—and she feared for his safety. She prepared lunch with movements that were entirely automatic, alarmed when he did not turn up for that meal either.

'Jake,' she said, when the rest of the men had gone, 'I really do think we ought to do something.'

'Aye.' He scratched his head thoughtfully. 'It's unlike him to be missing for so long, but who's to say which direction he took. It would be like searching for a needle in a haystack. And he wouldn't thank us for going after him if he was after peace and quiet.'

'I don't care what he thinks,' she cried. 'I'm worried—I really am!'

Jake looked at her shrewdly. 'You've fallen for the guy, haven't you?'

Susi nodded miserably.

'You amaze me, you really do. I thought you hated his guts.'

She shrugged self-consciously. 'I'm surprised myself considering the way he's treated me. The trouble is it doesn't do me any good, especially as I'm Carl's sister. It was a black mark against me from the beginning. He'll never allow himself to get involved—I'm too much of a reminder.'

'It's a pity,' said Jake. 'Latham could do with a woman. It's not natural him shutting himself off from the outside world the way he does. Not that I was sorry when Alison left him—she was no good, no good at all. Full of her own importance, that one. It was his money she was after, I'm sure. But she wasn't so stupid that she didn't want the guy to look good too.'

'I'm sure Latham knows that,' said Susi. 'Was he very upset?'

The old man shrugged. 'Latham's not one for giving away his feelings, but I reckon it was his pride that was hurt most.'

'It's his pride that's hurt now.' Susi looked at him

sadly. 'We had a few words yesterday, and the fact that I refused to go riding didn't help. I couldn't believe he was holding out an olive branch. Can't we go after him, Jake?'

The lined face was compassionate. 'I know how you feel, but let's give him a bit more time. There's no sense in worrying yourself unduly. He'll turn up when he's ready.'

As if to prove his words the clatter of hooves came from the yard outside, and rushing to the door Susi saw Latham ride up. He looked dusty and weary, but there was nothing wrong with him that she could see. Rather than admit she had been concerned she turned back into the kitchen and when he followed a few minutes later was busy piling dishes into the dishwasher. There was one thing to be said for this house: it had every labour-saving device imaginable.

'Have you any lunch for me?'

The rapid question startled her, making her jerk quickly round, dropping one of the plates as she did so. Her eyes were wide and questioning, but she dared not ask where he had been. He wouldn't care whether she had been bothered by his absence or not.

Latham washed his hands at the sink and she was vitally conscious of the big bulk of his body so close to hers. The lines of strain and weariness seemed to be etched more deeply into his face. His clothes were dust-stained as though he had travelled hard and long.

She reached his meal out of the oven and placed it on the table, setting out a knife and fork and plenty of thick bread to mop up his gravy, which was what most of the men seemed to like.

She hovered a few yards away. There was really nothing left for her to do, but she felt reluctant to leave.

'Sit down, for pity's sake!'

Again his deep voice startled her. Obediently she slid on to the bench opposite him, her fingers twisting nervously in her lap beneath the table. It was stupid letting this man unnerve her.

'You said you would give me your answer today.' There was no emotion on his face, it was devoid of all expression, only the coal black of his eyes blazing out at her. 'Have you made up your mind?'

The rapid beats of her heart were painful in the extreme. They drummed a tattoo in her breast and she felt a pulse quivering nervously at the base of her throat. 'I'm not sure,' she said hesitantly.

'Do you want to stay?' His chin was thrust aggressively forward and he paused in the act of forking potatoes into his mouth.

'I had a feeling *you* might have changed *your* mind.' Susi looked at him probingly. 'After the way you reacted yesterday I thought perhaps you wouldn't want me anywhere near you.'

'You really think I'm that stupid? God, Susi, that has nothing to do with me asking you to work for me. They're two entirely separate things. What I'm asking for is a business relationship, nothing else.'

Susi felt as though she had been plunged into ice. Why had he invited her out yesterday if that was all he had in mind? Unless of course it was simply the fact that she had touched his face that had spoiled everything. It had certainly had a traumatic effect on Latham. She could understand how he felt. She had touched a very vulnerable part of him. The shock to his system must have been absolute.

And now he was making it clear that she would never get another opportunity to get close to him. She swallowed painfully, unaware that her anguish showed in her eyes.

'I never thought it would be anything else,' she said, with a hint of defiance. 'But twelve months is a long time to tie myself down. I'm not sure I'd want to stay here that long. After all, it's not the sort of work that I've trained for.'

'Oh yes, I was forgetting.' The corners of his lips turned down in a sneer. 'We mustn't waste your valuable qualifications, must we?'

'I don't think I asked for that.' Susi felt like scratching his eyes out. She hated anyone making fun of her chosen profession.

His smile was cynical. 'Twelve months is the stipulated time. Either you stay, or you go now. Suit yourself.'

Susi found it difficult to believe that he was giving her an ultimatum. She had been under the impression that he wanted her to stay, that he would be disappointed if she said no. Now it appeared he couldn't care less. Her heart fell like a stone to the bottom of her stomach. It looked as though he had done some hard thinking while he was out—perhaps that was the reason he had gone? It could even be that he regretted asking her to stay, that he was hoping she would say no.

She looked at him warily. 'I'm still not sure.'

'God, I can't stand women who don't know their own minds!' He glared angrily. 'I could have sworn yesterday that you'd say yes. What's brought about this change of heart?'

You, she wanted to say. You've done this to me. You and your damn stupid arrogant manner. But that would get her nowhere at all. 'Like I said, I'd be wasting my training.'

He banged the table with his fist. 'You're a woman, Susi, for pity's sake, not a man! Why the hell did you pick a career like that?'

She looked at him coldly. 'It's what I wanted. It was what my father did.'

'Then Carl should have followed in his footsteps, not you,' he snapped. 'What was he good at? You tell me. He could turn his hands to most things, but he was expert at nothing. It was him your father should have helped, not you.'

'When I want your opinion, Mr Elliot, I'll ask for it!' Susi was consumed with a burning rage. This conversation was getting her nowhere. She bounced up from the seat and stormed over to the kitchen door.

'I take it,' he said narrowly, 'that this means you're leaving? A pity. You've proved an excellent house-keeper, coping with the job of secretary better than I ever expected. It's been a relief to have the paperwork taken off my hands. It now looks as though I'll have to put myself back into harness. There's no way I could allow another woman here.'

Whether his words had been chosen intentionally Susi did not know, but she could not ignore his unspoken plea. She looked at him with resignation on her face. 'I'll stay, Latham,' adding beneath her breath, Damn you! It will be the hardest thing I've ever done, but I'll stay because I love you. You'll never know that, but I do.

She was glad he could not hear her thoughts, but even so he looked relieved. He did not actually smile but she could see that he was pleased, 'Your duties will start from tomorrow,' he said.

Slowly Susi walked back towards him. 'Am I to be given any free time? Will I be allowed out by myself?'

His eyes narrowed suspiciously. 'Are you asking me whether you'll have time to search for Carl? I thought you'd given up on that. Wasn't it your intention to return to England?'

'You're trying to confuse me,' she accused bitterly. 'I'm merely asking what my rights are.'

'Shall we say you'll be here to do the work when there's work to be done?' he said coldly. 'The rest of the time will be your own.'

'I don't find that satisfactory.' She eyed him haughtily. 'I want proper hours. I'm entitled to that.'

Latham shrugged, mouth tight. 'I don't see that we can fix any set hours when you've two jobs rolled into one. Mrs Riley was on full-time call.'

'Mrs Riley didn't do your office work,' snapped Susi. 'She had time to herself.'

'What time do you usually start getting breakfast?' He settled back in his seat and studied her face closely.

'Eight o'clock,' she admitted.

'And what time is our evening meal finished?'

'About eight again, I suppose.'

'They are your hours, then,' he said cuttingly. 'Plus, of course, the meals at weekends.'

'Twelve hours a day?' Susi exclaimed. 'How much are you going to pay me for all that?'

'Enough,' he replied crisply. 'Are you suggesting you can't cope?'

'It's no more than I've been used to these last weeks,' she returned strongly, green eyes flashing. 'I can cope, if it's worth my while.'

'I'll make sure of that,' he said. 'I've been called many things in my time, but never mean. It's worth it to me, Susi, to pay you well. You do a good job.'

Praise indeed! But if he paid her as well as he intimated then it would not be long before she could save enough to buy herself a car. Then she would no longer be a prisoner. She would be able to go out in her free time, which would certainly be minimal, but even so it would be good to get away from this place occasionally.

It was a relief when he finally let her go. She went to her room wondering whether she had done the right thing. Anything could happen in twelve months and if she and Latham did not enjoy any happier a relationship than they were at this moment it would not be a very pleasurable period in her life. It would drag interminably. And she still hadn't found out where he had been!

When she went into the office the next morning Latham was waiting with her contract. She felt bitter. He was certainly making sure she did not back out. She read it through carefully, noting that it would be impossible to leave before the twelve-month period was up. If she signed she could blame no one but herself. He was putting no pressure on her—except emotionally— and he was not aware of that.

But sign it she did, as she had known she would. When he left her five minutes later she was resigned to a whole new future.

Things changed when she became Latham's proper employee. He treated her in a very businesslike manner. There were no picnics. There were orders issued and she was expected to carry them out. But he no longer complained when she used the pool—in her own time, of course—which was usually during the evenings, sometimes after lunch when she took an hour off before beginning work in the office again.

The attitude of his other employees changed too. Whereas before the men had been reluctant to approach her, apparently warned off by Latham, they now started chatting to her, and in fact became quite friendly. Latham frowned on all this but said nothing. If he had Susi would have told him where to get off!

Nor could she stop thinking about Carl. It disturbed her that he did not want to see her, and she knew that the day would come when she would try once again to find him.

Two weeks passed and she still had had no chance to enjoy any free time away from Kalabara. The money Latham paid her was more than generous, though, and she knew that it would not take long to save up for the promised car—then there would be no stopping her.

And then, unexpectedly, Latham said to her one day, 'You deserve a break, Susi. Jake can cook the meals tomorrow. I'll take you into the Blue Mountains.'

She could not hide her surprise. 'What have I done to deserve this?'

'You've proved yourself,' came the staggering reply, 'and there's an old friend of mine who lives in Katoomba that I have to call on.'

'I'm honoured you even thought of me,' she said, feeling the sudden painful thud of her heart.

He looked at her, an odd expression in his black eyes. 'There are not many girls I know who would have worked as hard as you and not complained. You're quite a remarkable person.'

Their eyes met and held for several long seconds. Susi was the first to look away, trying desperately to ignore her racing pulses. There was something in the way Latham looked at her which suggested he was not as immune to her as he made out—unless it was wishful thinking on her part! It could be that. It very likely was.

Since she had discovered that she loved him he had been farther away from her than ever. Their relationship had been on a strictly business basis. He had given her orders and she had carried them out, and they were the only occasions he spoke to her. Whenever she swam in the pool he was conspicuous by his absence, always choosing times when she was not there to use it himself.

It was obvious what he was doing and Susi felt

desperately hurt. From her bedroom window she could
see a corner of the pool and more than once, usually
after dark, she saw Latham standing at the edge,
unaware that she watched.

The artificial lights that illuminated the area turned
his bronzed skin even darker and from that distance it
was impossible to see the scars. But it was not
impossible to check her reaction at seeing him half-
naked. She was like a lovesick schoolgirl instead of a
mature woman of twenty-two, she told herself, but still
could not refrain from trying to catch glimpses of him.

They were the only occasions when he was relaxed,
when he was himself, and they were moments she would
have liked to share. It saddened her that he had
withdrawn back into his shell.

But now he had held out the hand of friendship once
again, and this time she was determined not to make a
wrong move.

CHAPTER SIX

THE day could not go quickly enough, and Susi was far too excited to sleep that night. It was stupid, she knew, when Latham probably had nothing more in mind than giving her a break from her daily routine. Certainly he would not use it as an excuse to seduce her.

She found it entirely amazing that he could go so long without a woman. A man of his virility must surely feel frustrated—and yet she knew there was no one else. He never went away from the stud. He spent the whole of his day seeing to the horses.

Susi was not quite sure how he managed to find sufficient work to keep him occupied. There was, of course, the necessary job of making sure the visiting mares were settled in, that they were not upset or nervous or alarmed in any way. Some of the mares were highly strung and needed careful handling, and on these occasions Latham looked after them himself, unwilling to leave the job to any of his hands, no matter how expert they were.

And there was always the job of keeping the stables clean and sweet-smelling, a never-ending, thankless task that was done uncomplainingly. The whole of the stud was kept in immaculate order, repairs being carried out at all times so that there was never a broken fence or loose nail on which the horses might harm themselves.

Susi suspected that the part Latham liked best was exercising the horses. He was up early each morning, taking the biggest and boldest stallions for himself. They were tricky to handle, she had seen some of them playing up, but always Latham showed them who was master.

Unsure what to put on for their trip to the Blue Mountains, but as it was another of those incredibly hot days with which Australia was blessed, Susi decided on a pair of white shorts and a brief lemon sun-top, tying up her hair to keep it out of her nape, slipping an uncrushable skirt into her bag to pop on when they visited Latham's friend.

As she made her way out to his waiting car her heart skittered painfully. This was a day to remember, she promised herself. She must do nothing to spoil it.

Latham looked devastating in cream linen pants and shirt, the pale colours emphasising the depth of his tan. The smile that he gave her was warm and appraising, and as she slid on to the seat beside him the heat that she felt had nothing to do with the temperature of the day.

She was more aware than ever of her love for this man, and it was all she could do to stop herself from leaning towards him and giving him a kiss. She wondered what his reaction would be.

Instead she concentrated on her surroundings. As on previous occasions when they had driven through the Australian countryside she became aware of the vastness of it all. They drove for miles and miles without a change in scenery, whereas in England there was always something different round the next corner. She privately decided that she liked England better, it felt cosier, wrapping itself about one where this vast continent seemed impersonal, caring little for the individual.

Soon they were on the Western Highway, and although they travelled in silence Susi was by no means uncomfortable. There was no atmosphere between them today. She enjoyed viewing the various places that they passed through in Latham's open-topped car, the towns with their narrow streets and fine parks, a reservoir which Latham told her used to supply water to Sydney until the present dam was built.

'The Blue Mountains,' he informed her, as they began to climb noticeably, 'were at one time impenetrable. There was no road where we are now. Several early explorers from Sydney came along the valleys until they reached the mountains, but were driven back by sheer walls of rock rising a hundred feet.

'But it became imperative that they find a way across. The narrow strip of land on which the first settlers were living was no longer enough, especially when a severe drought in 1812 caused a loss of stock and subsequent food supplies. It was a certain Gregory Blaxland, encouraged by Governor Macquarie, who led an expedition and by sheer doggedness and determination found a way across.'

Susi was eager for information and listened avidly. She wanted to hear everything Latham could tell her about his country. He was proud of it, and rightly so. 'All these must be new towns, then?'

He nodded. 'The City of the Blue Mountains encompasses twenty-four different townships. Blaxland is one of them, named after the man himself. You'd love it in autumn—the trees are a blaze of colour. It's just like walking down an English street. Most of our trees stay green the whole year around.'

As they climbed Susi spotted flowering gums that swept into the ravine, a manor house at Faulconbridge that looked as though it belonged to England, and then they turned off the Highway and followed the Cliff Drive.

Through breaks in the clumps of trees on the

roadside Susi caught glimpses of the Megalong Valley,
and they came out at Narrow Neck Plateau where
Jamieson Valley appeared. She caught her breath at
sight of the sheer cliffs in pink and rust-coloured
sandstone lining the vast blue valley.

At Cyclorama Point they stopped. 'This is the highest
lookout at Katoomba,' Latham told her—and it was
indeed spectacular. They could see right along the
Megalong and Jamieson Valleys. Latham pointed out
the steep cliffs of Narrow Neck, and the Ruined Castle,
Saddleback and Mount Solitary. 'Visibility is not so
good today,' he said, 'but on a clear day you can see
Mount Jellore at Mittagong in one direction and the
sands at Botany Bay in the other—a distance of more
than ninety kilometres.'

Susi could well believe it.

They continued their cliff drive until they reached
Echo Point, the main tourist spot. Susi gazed in awe at
feathery green vegetation, at flowering gums, pines and
purple buddleia. But it was the three massive jagged
rocks that were attracting everyone's attention. 'Why
are they called the Three Sisters?' she asked.

Latham grinned. 'Legend has it that there once lived
three aboriginal sisters, Meenhi, Wimlah and
Gunnedoo. Their father was a witch doctor named
Tyawan. They were very very happy, as was everyone
who lived in the Blue Mountains. They were afraid of
only one creature—the Bunyip, a mythical monster who
lived in a deep hole.'

Susi began to laugh. It didn't sound like the Latham
she knew, to relate a fairy story like this. But when he
stopped she urged him to go on. 'I'm interested, I really
am. It's just not what I expected.'

'Every day the girl's father had to pass by the
Bunyip's hole to collect food,' he continued, his face as

solemn as he could make it in the light of Susi's scepticism. 'And so that his daughters would be safe he used to leave them high on a cliff behind a rocky wall.

One day a big centipede appeared on top of the cliff and frightened Meenhi. She threw a stone at it, but it rolled over the cliff and crashed into the valley, awakening the Bunyip instead.'

'He came after them, I suppose?' Susi's vivid imagination saw the three girls recoiling in horror.

Latham nodded. 'The noise of the falling stone stopped the birds, animals and fairies singing, split open the rock, and left the sisters on a narrow ledge.

'Tyawan heard his daughters crying and looked up in time to see the Bunyip lurching at them. Quick as a flash he pointed his magic bone and turned them to stone, intending to change them back afterwards. But the Bunyip, angry that he had been outsmarted, rounded on the witch doctor instead. He ran away, but found himself trapped against a big rock, so he turned himself into a lyrebird and flew into a small cave.'

'And they were all safe?' Susi found herself actually believing this story.

'Not really,' said Latham. 'The Bunyip went back to his hole, but Tyawan couldn't find his magic bone so was unable to turn his daughters back to their natural selves. He's still searching, watched by the three sisters on their mountain ledge, hoping he'll find it one day.' He paused, a hand to his ear. 'Listen, can you hear the lyrebird calling as he searches for his lost bone?'

Susi laughed, wishing Latham was always this entertaining. 'What an enchanting story—and since you're such a mine of information, tell me why are the mountains so blue?'

'A scientific phenomenon,' he said, 'The haze is caused by rays of light striking dust particles and small droplets of moisture in the atmosphere. This is especially effective here because of the oil evaporating from the eucalyptus trees, but it's by no means confined to these mountains only—although some people claim this is so.'

Then Susi spotted a cable car swinging over the valley and turned to him impulsively. 'Oh, we must go on that!'

Latham smiled. 'Are you sure you won't be scared? It's pretty high up—two hundred and seventy-five metres above the valley floor.'

'I'd love it,' she returned confidently, so they made their way to the starting point, waiting on the platform until the Scenic Skyway swung back to unload its passengers.

They climbed on board and it moved slowly across the mountain gorge. Susi held her breath for the first few seconds, her heart rising to her mouth, but soon she got used to the exciting feeling of being suspended in space.

There were excellent views of Katoomba Falls, The Three Sisters and Orphan Rock. 'Orphan Rock,' explained Latham with a wicked grin, 'is reputedly the beautiful younger sister of Meenhi, Wimlah and Gunnedoo. They were very jealous of her and pushed her out—and there she is—all alone.'

It was not until they had reached the other side of the valley that Susi realised she was clutching Latham's arm as though her life depended on it. He had his other arm protectively about her shoulders, holding her comfortingly against him. There was something remarkably erotic about being so close to him in this wonderful world of space.

She would never forget this occasion, and when he lowered his head, pressing his lips to her brow, she looked up at him with wide wondering eyes, unaware that they were as green as the valley below. 'Enjoying it?' he asked softly.

Susi nodded, too choked with emotion for words. It was a beautiful, beautiful experience being carried across the gorge, made even more memorable by Latham's presence. His attunement to her feelings, his gentleness—they were all something she had not shared before. She was not accustomed to him treating her like this and she intended making the most of it, snuggling closer on the return journey, rewarded by a tightening of his hand about her shoulders.

'Are you frightened?'

'A little,' she admitted, 'but more thrilled than anything else. It's like being in a different world. I'm glad you brought me, I really am. I do appreciate you taking time off to show me these sights.'

'Like I said, you deserve it,' he smiled. 'You're a real little trooper and no mistake. I suppose I ought to thank Carl for bringing you to me.'

Susi wished he had not mentioned her brother's name. He cast a shadow over this flawless day. 'Oh, look,' she exclaimed, her attention suddenly diverted. 'There's a scenic railway. Can we go on that as well?'

Latham chuckled. 'You're a devil for punishment! Are you sure your stomach can take it?'

If it could stand his nearness it could stand anything, she thought. The blood pounding through her veins, drumming in her head, was certainly not caused by the smooth journey of the cable car. She was more aware of him than she had ever been and wanted this day to go on for ever. 'It can take it,' she said quietly.

'Alison's couldn't,' he returned surprisingly. 'She wouldn't even set foot in this aerial car, even though it's perfectly safe and is maintained at a very high standard. I remember when I brought her here she said if I didn't mind her bringing her dinner up all over me then she would come. I never asked her again.'

Susi wondered why he had introduced Alison into the conversation. This woman, more than Carl, ruined her pleasure. She hated to think of Latham with anyone else, especially that bitch! It was with difficulty that she pushed all thoughts of the blonde girl from her mind.

As soon as they returned to their starting point they joined the queue for the Scenic Railway. When the car dipped over the edge of the valley Susi thought she was going to leave her stomach behind. It was a thrill she would never forget, far more scary than the gentle movement of the cable car. Alison would certainly never have survived this! Susi clutched Latham and they laughed into each other's eyes as his arm came protectively about her.

The rail car proceeded into a tunnel cut out of solid rock, quickly opening into a narrow canyon with a remarkable view of the mountains. On either side were sheer sandstone walls, and as they emerged into daylight the descent was so steep that Susi closed her eyes, glad she had done so when Latham's arm tightened, drawing her even closer to him.

It was worth the trip just for this. There were no other circumstances in which he would hold her so close. She could even feel the beat of his heart against her side. It was nowhere near as erratic as her own—but surely faster than usual? Or was it wishful thinking? Who cared? This was a moment to relish, one that would remain in her memory for a long time.

As they neared the lower station they entered the dense growth of the bush with the lush whites, greens and purples of the gums, the wattles, and other infinite variety of trees that made up this rich carpet of vegetation.

At the bottom they got out and stretched their legs, viewing an abandoned coalmine with its rusted buckets and old cables. 'The first passengers on the railway,' explained Latham, 'were bushwalkers who came upon this coal mine accidentally. When they asked to be carried up in one of the skips the director of the mining company realised there could be a demand for passenger travel and had a special wooden skip built. It carried twelve passengers and was called the Mountain Devil, running only at weekends. When the coalmine closed the Government bought the railway for the tourists.'

Susi was not so sure she would have felt as calm in the wooden car as she had in the duralumin one which was as safe as modern skills could make it—or so she had been told. But then again, if she had had Latham with her who knew how she would have felt? Never had a man affected her so deeply. If he had suggested walking up the side of the valley, hacking their way through as the first explorers must have done, she would willingly have agreed. She would have followed him to the ends of the earth.

The vegetation changed as they walked through a rain forest, and Susi exclaimed anew over cabbage tree palms and brilliant red flame trees, and staghorn ferns growing high on tree trunks. It was a veritable wonderland. Birds of every different hue imaginable squabbled overhead, sunlight filtered in prismatic rays through the tracery of green. And Latham held her hand! The most magic part of it all.

After their trip they had lunch in one of the big hotels in Katoomba, Susi freshening herself up first in the ladies' powder room, putting on her skirt and brushing her hair until its thick shining length sat sleekly about her shoulders.

Latham had not commented on her appearance at all today, much to her inner chagrin, but the look on his face when she walked into the restaurant made her glad that she had taken the trouble to smarten herself up.

'You look good,' he murmured quietly when she sat down beside him, and just those few words were sufficient to set her adrenalin flowing.

Although it was an excellent meal Susi found it difficult to concentrate on the food. Her mind was totally occupied with Latham. The atmosphere in the restaurant was intimate enough for her to forget the other diners and make believe that she and Latham were alone.

Never had her heart raced so intermittently. It was like sporadic machine-gun fire within her breast and she knew that more than once Latham's eyes rested on the pulse fluttering nervously at the base of her throat.

She felt sure that he was attracted to her but was afraid to let her feelings show in case he was angry. He would think she was being nice to him out of pity—and that was something he could not stomach.

Nevertheless there was a distinct awareness between them that had never been there before—a physical thing that could not be denied by either of them. Latham, being the man that he was, though, controlled his feelings with a strength she could only admire. It was an unfortunate state of affairs, but not one that she could do anything about. Only time was on her side.

If she was careful not to do or say anything that Latham could possibly misconstrue then gradually there should develop between them a relationship that would be impossible for anyone to destroy. It would be built on complete trust and should last as long as either of them wanted.

Susi would have liked it to last for ever. Her love for

Latham grew daily and she was afraid that very soon she would be unable to hide her feelings any longer. At the moment it was imperative that she did so, even though she found the task much harder than she expected.

When his hand accidentally touched hers as he reached across the table to refill her wine glass it took every ounce of willpower not to flinch. The brush of his fingers shot shivers of sensation through her nerve-stream and more than anything she would have liked him to turn that touch into a caress. She craved physical contact and knew that sooner or later he would see it in her eyes.

In one way it was a relief when the meal was over, in another Susi did not want these precious moments to end. It was rarely they got together like this, with Latham in such a good mood that he treated her with none of his normal arrogance.

On the other hand they still had the rest of the day in front of them, and Susi intended making the most of it. It was a bittersweet experience, this day out with Latham, one that she would like to repeat. She was certainly going to do nothing to mar it.

Latham's friend lived in a big house in the heart of Katoomba. It was a splendid colonial-style building and she imagined it to be one of the first houses built when the town was developed.

Maxwell Vincent was a big bluff man with a deep ruddy complexion and the stature of an ox. His voice was loud and gruff, his hair and eyebrows white and wildly untameable. The hand which pumped Susi's was like a vice and she felt as though he was crushing her bones. 'Any friend of Latham's is a friend of mine,' he boomed.

'I'm not exactly his friend,' said Susi, rubbing her

fingers when he let go. 'I'm his housekeeper and
secretary rolled into one.'

Max's wide mouth pulled down admiringly. 'Lucky
you, Latham! Where did you find her? English, too.
What's happened to that woman Riley? You always
swore when she went you'd never have another woman
in the house. Changed your mind?' He looked at Susi
from beneath his straggly brows. 'Can't say I blame
you, mind—this one's a real humdinger!'

Without waiting for any answers to his questions he
took them through to the back of his house where there
was a big garden room—this was the only word Susi
could find to describe it. It was full of plants and cane
furniture, but where there would have been windows in
an English conservatory there was simply wire mesh, so
that although they could enjoy the fresh air they would
not be disturbed by flying insects. Max's housekeeper, a
thin wiry woman of indeterminate age, brought them a
tray of iced drinks.

'I'm bloody annoyed that you've had lunch out
instead of joining me.' Max frowned ferociously at
Latham. 'It's not on, is it? Especially when you always
insist I eat with you when I'm over your way. What
have I done? Or were you reluctant to share your young
lady? Is that it, eh?'

Susi felt herself blushing. Max was making it sound
as though she were Latham's private property, and
nothing was farther from the truth. If Max knew the
real reason behind her working for Latham he would
certainly have kept his mouth shut.

For a while the two men talked business. It appeared
Max also ran a stud farm, and they discussed how
things were going, whether the present recession was
having any effect, relating amusing anecdotes and
generally having a good chinwag.

Frequently Susi found Max looking at her with a curiously speculative expression, but it was not until they had been there for over an hour that he came out with the thoughts that were going through his mind.

'Know who this young lady reminds me of, Latham? That lad you had working for you—the one who turned sour.'

Susi glanced uncomfortably at Latham, growing warm, her traitorous heart beating fast yet again, but for an entirely different reason. For the first time she felt bitter towards Carl, feeling that she might get some of the blame for what he had done.

'Carl Kingswood?' asked Latham coolly. 'Do you think so?' He looked at Susi, as if seeing her through his friend's eyes.

Max shrugged his heavy shoulders. 'I could be wrong, of course. I saw the young villain the other day, you know that? He's a trucker now. Bit of a nerve, if you ask me. He must know someone will spot him.'

There was a sudden hardening of Latham's face, a narrowing of his cold eyes. 'Drive for himself, does he? Or is he working for one of the big companies?'

Susi knew that he was counting on Max's every word.

Max shook his head. 'I've no idea, mate. He was carrying a load of timber, but there was no name on the truck.'

'Why didn't you stop him? You know I'm after his hide!'

'I might be a big man,' laughed Max, 'but I'm not the Incredible Hulk. There was no way I could have stopped that truck. Even if I'd stood in the middle of the road I reckon he'd have run me down once he recognised me.'

Latham nodded resignedly. 'You're right, of course.

But let me know next time you see him. Maybe he's on a regular run. Keep your eyes open—there are a few things I want to settle with that guy.'

He glanced at Susi as he spoke, and her stomach churned uncomfortably. It was not pleasant having your own brother threatened, more especially when there was nothing she could do about it. She was grateful he had not mentioned to Maxwell that she was Carl's sister, but on the other hand it did not make things any easier for her.

One day Maxwell Vincent would find out. He would then wonder why nothing had been said on this occasion. It was a very delicate and unhealthy situation, one that she wished she had never got into.

She wondered whether her parents had ever guessed that all might not be well. Especially when the letters stopped. They had talked so often about coming out here, now she wondered whether they would have done so. Maybe it had all been a pipe-dream. There had certainly been no money saved towards it.

No parents would accept easily that their son was anything less than perfect. Or had they thought that they could sort him out? That with a loving and stable family behind him Carl might begin to make a success of his life? There was so much that they had withheld from her.

'I still think Susi bears a resemblance to Carl,' said Max. 'It's a bit of a coincidence, don't you think, Latham? Perhaps you'd better watch her!'

It was meant as a joke, but Susi felt insulted and shot Max an angry glance. Before she could speak, Latham went on, 'Susi is a sensitive girl, Max. You shouldn't say things like that. You've upset her.'

Instantly Maxwell Vincent's expression changed. 'Hell, girl, I didn't mean that. I wouldn't hurt you for the world. I respect Latham's judgment. He would never have employed you if he hadn't thought you were honest and trustworthy. I reckon he learned his lesson where Carl Kingswood was concerned. Even then he knew what he was taking on. It's a pity the lad didn't live up to the faith Latham had in him.'

With difficulty Susi remained silent, knowing that if she started she would be unable to stop. She would disclose the fact that Carl was her brother and would strongly defend him no matter that he was in the wrong. He was family, and family ties meant more to her than anything else.

Not until they were on their way home did she get the opportunity to thank Latham. 'I appreciate you not letting Max know that I was Carl's sister.'

'It was the least I could do,' he said gruffly. 'I knew you'd get on your high horse defending that no-good brother of yours, and I had no wish to drag Maxwell into our arguments. But it was good to hear that Carl is still in New South Wales. I feel so much more confident about our paths meeting. I might get my revenge sooner than expected.'

There was a gleam in his eye that angered Susi. 'I can just imagine you with your big hands round his throat, your thumbs pressed against his windpipe, squeezing until there's no life left in him! You'd enjoy that, wouldn't you?' Her eyes blazed with sudden anger.

'It would be no more than he deserved,' came the grim rejoinder.

'When you talk like this, Latham, I don't think I like you very much.' There was distaste on her face as she spoke, even though inside she felt as though her heart were bleeding.

'Have you ever?' he asked sharply. 'But you knew all this before you decided to stay. Don't make things more difficult for yourself by dragging Carl into the conversation every time we speak.'

'It wasn't my fault Maxwell Vincent saw him,' she burst out. 'Believe me, it was the last thing I wanted to hear!'

'Last?' A thick brow rose quizzically. 'I didn't know you'd given up the idea of trying to find him.'

'You know what I mean,' she blazed. 'But let me tell you this—you lay a finger on my brother and I shall have the police on you before you have time to bat an eyelid! I'm not trying to defend Carl. If he's done wrong he deserves all he has coming to him, but it's not up to you to hand out that punishment.'

He stiffened noticeably and there was no sign now of the rapport that had existed between them. The few words that Maxwell Vincent had unwittingly dropped out had ruined the whole day. Susi had been so careful not to do or say anything out of place, never expecting this stranger to destroy their fragile relationship in one fell swoop.

The journey seemed interminable, the atmosphere electric. Susi was afraid to speak in case they argued some more, and Latham himself made no attempt to say anything.

She feared for Carl's safety more now than she had at any time during her weeks in Australia. Maxwell's unfortunate sighting had brought Latham's hatred flooding back to the surface. She had only to look at him to see the dull flush to his cheeks, the venom behind those tightly drawn lips.

It became imperative that she find Carl and warn him. He would not thank her for doing so, he already knew Latham was after his blood, but she must impress on him that it was more important than ever that he keep out of his way. He should have had more sense than to remain so close.

On the other hand, it might have been a one-off trip that he had made. He might not be living anywhere near and it had been mere coincidence that he had driven past Maxwell Vincent's place. He could be living in Melbourne or Brisbane, or anywhere in the whole vast continent. Only Alison could help her find out.

Now that she had more freedom it should not be too difficult to manage a day in Sydney. She would call on this woman again and not be put off until she got Carl's address. She had a right to it. She wondered why Alison was afraid of Carl, whether he had ever threatened her. Who was saying how his character had developed? Meeting Carl would be like meeting a stranger.

Distaste over the whole affair rose like poison in her throat and she clenched her fists tightly, wondering if there was ever going to be any escape from this madness that had infiltrated into her life.

And then she realised that becoming angry with Latham would get her nowhere. He would give her no opportunity to drive into Sydney. He would keep her as much a prisoner as she had ever been. It was far, far better to keep on the right side of him and, if the truth was known, it was what she wanted anyway.

So instead of sitting glaring she forced herself to smile, a tentative smile, but one nevertheless. 'I'm sorry,' she said, 'I shouldn't have spoken like that. I know how you feel about Carl, and it's understandable that you're bitter towards him. I expect I'd be the same if I were in your shoes, but you must understand how I feel too. He is my brother after all, and it was Carl I came out here to find. But I had no right speaking to you like that.'

He glanced across and to her surprise pulled into the side of the road and stopped, half turning in his seat and looking at her with suspicion. 'I wish I could believe your apology was sincere.'

'What makes you think it isn't?' she asked crossly. It had been an effort to apologise and she resented his flinging it back in her face.

'Because, whenever we talk about Carl, you take umbrage. You would never back down.'

'I haven't backed down now. I just felt that I owed you an apology—and thought you would accept it.' She was careful to keep her eyes on his face as she spoke.

Suddenly the aggression went out of him, a slow smile softening his angular features. 'I do believe you, Susi. It's that fool Max I should be mad at for ruining our perfect day.'

Susi's eyes widened. 'You thought it perfect?'

He grinned. 'It was more perfect than any other we've spent together.'

An admission indeed! It was unlike Latham to say anything like this. 'Then we're—friends again?' Her eyes pleaded unconsciously.

Latham shook his head as though he was a lost man. 'You have a way of getting to me, Susi. God knows what it is about you. You make me forget myself. You're the one person I'm beginning to relax with, though why that should be the case when you're Carl's sister, I'll never be able to understand. I never thought I'd feel easy with a woman again.'

The pound of her heartbeats echoed in Susi's head, and her mouth went suddenly dry. She looked at Latham, her lips parted, her breathing rapid and shallow. 'I'm glad,' she whispered. It was all she could say, but it was enough, for with a groan Latham took her into his arms.

'Oh, Susi, Susi,' he muttered, his mouth seeking hers.

The sweetness of his kiss sent Susi's blood racing and

she arched herself closer, linking her hands round his neck, giving herself to him, for the moment oblivious to everything except this man who was sending her crazy. Desire coursed through her, singing along her veins, pounding in her head. Her heart hammered wildly, painfully, and there was music in her ears.

Latham's lips feverishly explored the responsive sweetness of her mouth, and against her breast she felt the wild clamourings of his heart. His breathing was as deep and erratic as her own, his hands moulding her to him, his mouth urgent and insistent on hers.

Susi wished they were in his house instead of here in his car on the highway where passing traffic was being given a free show. Horns tooted encouragingly in the background, but she scarcely noticed them. This was the moment she had hoped for for a long time and she would not have cared had they been standing in the middle of a room full of strangers.

Latham had forgotten that he had labelled himself an undesirable man. He needed her, and the passion behind his kisses told her that he was in danger of releasing the emotions he had kept pent up for the last two years.

Had they not been in a public place she guessed he would have gone much further, for it was with reluctance that he finally put her from him. His eyes were glazed with a desire she was unused to seeing and his hands trembled as he framed her face, looking intently into her eyes.

'I'm sorry,' he said, 'but I just had to do that. I need you, Susi. I need you desperately.'

Susi found it difficult to speak. Her throat was dry, her mouth throbbing from the assault of his kiss. Her lips felt bruised and swollen. Never had she been in such a state. 'Don't apologise.' She sounded breathless, as though she had just run a four-minute mile. 'Oh, Latham, it was what I wanted too. It's a beautiful end to a beautiful day.'

'It's not over yet,' he said thickly. 'I want more, Susi. I want more of you—I want all of you. For God's sake, what are you doing to me?'

He looked anguished and Susi buried her head in his shoulder, sliding her arms round his back. She did not speak, she did not need to; her actions said it all.

With infinite gentleness Latham pushed her back into her seat, raking his still shaking hands through his hair, turning the key and starting the engine. 'This is madness. We must go before we make a spectacle of ourselves.'

Susi straightened her skirt, never for one second taking her eyes off his face. His scar was hidden from her, but it would not have mattered. She loved him unconditionally, and the sweetest part about it all was that it looked as though he was beginning to grow fond of her too.

He took several deep steadying breaths before putting the car into gear and pulling back out on to the highway. Susi rested her hand on his thigh and felt his muscles tense at her touch. She needed to maintain physical contact, to reassure him that she was as willing a partner as he to this whole affair.

She could not wait for them to reach Kalabara, knowing instinctively that he would start up again where he had left off. Ths time there would be no holds barred. They would be in complete privacy and—she could think no further. Her heart felt as though it was going to explode, and she tensed her stomach muscles as she tried to control the erotic thoughts that were racing through her mind.

Oh, Latham, she said to herself, I do love you. I do

want you. Please, please, don't spoil this thing for me. Don't change. Don't back away now.

More than once he glanced towards her, his smile tender and loving, telling her clearly that he still wanted her, that his need was as great as her own.

The journey seemed never-ending, but at last they turned off the road and down the track that led to the stud. If it were possible Susi's heart raced even more quickly, her pulses hammered, each and every one of her senses attuned to this man beside her. Impulsively she leaned over and pressed her lips to his cheek, drinking in the faint lingering odour of his after-shave, hungering for him, needing him.

He caught her face with his hand, holding it against him, kissing her hair, before turning his attention back to his driving and negotiating the final turn that took them into the yard.

It was a tremendous shock to see a strange car parked there. No one ever came here uninvited and visitors were the last thing she wanted at this moment. She was quite sure Latham felt the same way too.

After looking at the classy car for several seconds she turned enquiringly towards him, wondering whether he had any idea as to who his caller might be.

The change in him was dramatic, more so because it was unexpected. His face had blanched, lips grown white and thin. Gone was the man who only minutes earlier had excited her with unspoken promises.

She touched his arm anxiously. 'What is it, Latham?'

He glanced at her and she was shocked by the haunted quality of his eyes. Whoever his visitor it was clear he was not welcome.

CHAPTER SEVEN

'ALISON!' Latham's voice was hoarse. 'What the hell does she want? I haven't seen her since that day she walked out. Neither do I want to.' He gripped the wheel so tightly that his knuckles gleamed white. He was visibly shaking, and Susi silently cursed the other woman for turning up like this.

'How do you know?' she asked gently, wanting to reach out and touch him but afraid he might reject her. 'You haven't seen her in two years. How can you be so sure the car's hers?'

He glanced at her sharply, testily. 'I saw it that day I took you to her flat. It's Alison, make no mistake about that. But why has she come here now, that's what I want to know?' He made no attempt to move although they had been sitting there for a full minute. 'I refuse to see her!'

If the truth was known Susi did not want him to either, but they could not turn the car round and go. Alison would have seen their arrival through one of the windows. She was probably wondering even now what was keeping them.

'Perhaps it's business?' she said hesitantly, 'or maybe she's come to see me? Perhaps Carl's changed his mind.' She could not contain her sudden excitement, and jumped out of the car without waiting for Latham. All thoughts of what they had been going to do fled. She raced into the house, finding Alison in the comfortable air-conditioned lounge. She felt hot and clammy, and it irritated her that this woman looked coolly elegant.

Alison glanced at Susi coldly down the length of her perfect nose. 'Where on earth have you two been? I've waited simply hours!'

Susi still felt buoyant as a result of Latham's lovemaking, and even this woman's arrogant manner failed to dampen her spirits. Plus the fact that she might have brought news of Carl! 'You should have let us know you were coming. It's the first day Latham and I have had off. Is it Carl you've come about? Is he ready to see me? Have you brought his address?'

Alison tilted her chin that much higher, her eyes as cold and indifferent as she could make them. 'I didn't come all this way to pass a message on to you,' she said haughtily. 'It's Latham I want to see. Where is he?'

Susi looked behind her, realising for the first time that he had not followed her into the house. 'He's coming.' A choking feeling rose in her throat. Why would Alison want to see Latham after all this time?

An unbidden thought leapt to the surface of her mind, and she searched the other woman's face, looking for some clue that would tell her what she was thinking was not true.

But the satisfied smile she saw confirmed her suspicions. Alison visibly preened herself. 'I've been thinking a lot about Latham since that day you came to see me. You could be right—perhaps I was hasty. I've decided to see for myself what sort of a mess your brother made of his face.'

Susi felt every vestige of happiness drain from her. Although Latham professed to hate this woman who had cast him to one side, he had once loved her enough to consider marrying her. There was no reason why he should not fall in love with her all over again. Especially if Alison proved to him that her fears had been unfounded, that his scars no longer mattered.

She felt devastated as she gazed at Alison, her green eyes wide, her mouth hanging open.

'Shocked you, have I?' asked Alison nastily. 'I guess you never expected this. Making a play for him yourself, were you? I'm not surprised. He's a very attractive man, at least he was before your brother got at him. I must admit I can't wait to see what he looks like now.'

'He won't want to see you,' snapped Susi with more conviction than she felt. 'I think it stinks, what you did to him! I also think you have a nerve coming here. You won't get round him. You burned your boats when you walked out. If I were you I'd go before he makes mincemeat of you.'

'Hark who's talking!' There was a flash of blue from Alison's eyes. 'You have no reason to talk, after what your brother did.'

'Can I help that?' snapped Susi. 'I can't take the blame.'

'I doubt Latham sees it in quite that light,' returned Alison. 'You're forgetting how well I know him. He probably thinks that one Kingswood is as good as another.'

How true that was, thought Susi. But not any longer. He had changed towards her now. They had something really good going for them—so long as this hateful woman did not spoil it!

'Lord knows what you've done to get him on your side,' the blonde continued cattily. 'But don't build up your hopes too high. Now I'm here Latham will have eyes for no one else.'

At that moment Susi heard movement behind her and knew that Latham had entered the room. She was afraid to look at him, watching Alison's face instead.

The woman was a better actress than Susi gave her

credit for. Only by the merest tightening of her facial muscles did she give away the fact that Latham's scar disturbed her. Almost instantly she was all smiles, walking towards him, stopping only when he said harshly, 'Alison! What are you doing here?'

Susi knew she ought to leave them alone, but her feet were rooted to the spot and she watched the scene that unfolded before her eyes as though it was a play being acted on a stage.

'Latham darling, I couldn't keep away any longer.' Alison's false tones sickened Susi. 'I've been a bitch, and I know it.' There was even a tremor in her voice. 'But I've come to my senses at last.'

'You mean you've come to see what I look like?' Latham's face was impassive. 'Well, here I am—take a good hard look.' He thrust his scarred cheek towards her.

Alison laughed brittly, looking slightly shaken. 'But I know what you look like, darling—Susi told me. In fact it was Susi's doing that I'm here now. I suppose we should thank her. She made me realise how selfish I've been.' She took two more steps towards him. 'Darling, can you ever forgive me?'

Heavens! thought Susi, how false could you get? She hoped Latham would see through the act. If he showed signs of weakening she would never stand it.

Latham glanced across at her and Susi managed a weak smile. She had never seen quite such a sickened expression on a man's face before. She wondered what he was thinking, whether he was wondering if he ought to give Alison a second chance, or whether she had really ruined all that she had had going for her by walking out as he lay in his hospital bed.

'I'm quite sure,' he said strongly, 'that Susi had no intention of making you feel guilty. She's very outspoken. If she told you what she thought of you then it was me she was trying to protect.'

Alison looked suddenly unsure of herself, glancing across at Susi, flashing her a glance so full of venom and hatred that Susi flinched. But the next second Alison was in control of herself again, looking at Latham with a beautiful well rehearsed smile that Susi knew she thought irresistible.

'Whatever lay behind Susi's words, Latham, it brought me to my senses. I've been a fool. I can see now for myself that you're not half so disfigured as I feared.' Again she looked at Susi and then back to Latham. 'Perhaps, darling, we could talk this thing over in private?'

Susi swallowed a constricting lump in her throat, and she turned to leave the room, her legs feeling like lead. But as she walked past Latham he grabbed her. 'Whatever has to be said between us, Alison, Susi can hear. She's become a very good friend.'

'I see.' The woman compressed her scarlet lips. 'Does that mean you and I have no hope of resuming our relationship?'

'It means,' said Latham coldly, 'that you're not wanted here. When you walked out on me, Alison, I swore to myself that I'd never take you back. I meant it then and I'm of the same mind now.'

He still held Susi's arm, his fingers biting mercilessly. She wanted to cry out but gritted her teeth instead. 'I really think, Latham, that you ought to see Alison alone.'

'You could be right, Susi.' He caught her face between his hands, looking deep into her eyes. 'There are things that need clearing up. But don't forget that we have unfinished business.' He smiled briefly, the first smile Susi had seen since they arrived back.

'I'll be waiting,' she whispered huskily, before resolutely marching out of the room, closing the door quietly, feeling like banging it but knowing this would get her nowhere. She wanted to scream at Alison, demand that she leave now, but Latham had looked very sure when he said he would see her later, and she had every confidence in him. It was unlikely Alison would persuade him to change his mind.

It seemed an age before Alison left, and even then Latham did not come to her room. Up until then Susi had not realised how much she had hung on to his words. She could understand, though, that he would need a breathing space after his no doubt painful discussion with his former girl-friend.

She freshened herself with a shower, slipping into a pretty pink cotton sundress tied on the shoulders with shoe-string straps, then left her room in search of Latham. If he wouldn't come to her, then she would go to him.

She discovered him in his study, sitting at his desk, very much in the same position as she had found him on that first occasion. The moment she saw his face her spirits dropped and she knew there would be no further lovemaking between them that day.

He did not even look up when she entered, staring blankly at the desk. Not until she spoke his name did he seem to realise that she was in the room.

'How did things turn out?' she asked timidly, holding her breath as she waited for his reply.

His black eyes were dead. It was difficult to believe that there had been intense desire in their depths less than an hour earlier. 'Alison wants to take up where we left off.' There was resignation on his face and he avoided her eyes.

Susi's heart sank to the bottom of her stomach. 'And

what did you say?' Her whole future hinged on his answer.

He swallowed and she watched his Adam's apple go up and down, saw the tension in his fingers as they gripped the arms of the chair. 'I've agreed to give it a try.' He did not sound exactly enamoured with the situation.

Susi could not believe that she had heard him correctly. 'Why? For heaven's sake, why, after all she's done to you?' A sharp physical pain stabbed in her throat.

'She explained that she'd jumped the gun, that she had always wanted to come and see me but had been afraid of my reaction.' He still did not look at her.

'And you believed her?' Susi was livid. 'It seems strange to me that she waited until I came on the scene. Are you sure it isn't jealousy? That although she doesn't want you she's going to make darn sure no one else gets you either? You're a fool if you've let her take you in!'

His face tightened as he pushed himself jerkily up. Striding over to her, he gripped her shoulders brutally. 'You don't understand, Susi. I've known Alison a long time, I——'

She broke away angrily, despairingly. 'I understand only too well, Latham. My God, you had me going good and proper! Now I see that it wasn't me you wanted at all, it was a woman, *any woman*. Yet all the time you were hankering after Alison. It's Alison who still holds the strings to your heart. She only had to crook her little finger for you to go running. You make me sick!'

'Susi, please!' There was anguish on his face, but she refused to believe that it was sincere. 'Please try to understand.'

'Understand what?' she snapped cruelly. 'That you're

glad the waiting is over? Sheer hell these last two years have been, have they, waiting for Alison to come to her senses? If you thought that much of her why didn't you go to her? Answer me that, will you?'

He shook his head slowly, his brow furrowed with pain. 'It's not like that at all.'

Susi glared at him coldly, bleeding inside. 'If she means that much to you she can look after your house as well, and do your damn typing, because I'm going. No way am I going to remain here after the fool you've made of me!'

His jaw tightened, muscles jerking like mad, his lips drawn into a thin straight line. 'I think you're forgetting your contract, Susi. Twelve months was the stipulated time, and twelve months it will be.'

She could not believe it. He was insane! 'You bastard!' she cried. 'How dare you do this to me! If you think I'm going to remain here and see you fawning all over that coarse little bitch you're mistaken—I'm going now, and there's no way you can stop me!' Tears stung the back of her eyes and she hurled herelf out of the room before she broke down.

But as usual Latham was quicker, his hands clamping her shoulders, spinning her to face him. She opened her mouth to protest, but found it caught beneath his, his hard hands imprisoning her face.

Susi had wanted his kisses, but not in this manner, and she kicked his shins and pummelled his chest, all to no avail.

His kiss was brutal, punishing, demanding, violating her but at the same time creating an aching desire. Her chest heaved as she fought for control, hating him and loving him at the same time, wanting him but knowing she must reject him. Fighting Latham was one of the hardest things she had ever had to do, but fight him she must. She had lost him to Alison. All he was doing now was trying to save his own face.

When it became clear that in no circumstances was he going to let her go Susi toyed with the idea of kneeing him where it hurt, but then rejected it in favour of submitting quietly. It was a more ladylike way of doing things. Even so she remained mutely submissive, standing as still and cool as a statue, ignoring her pulses racing fit to burst, her heart crashing maniacally against her rib-cage. She had lost Latham before she had truly won him. Her affair had been shortlived in the extreme.

As soon as he realised that she was no longer fighting Latham let her go. 'I want you to promise me,' he said, 'that you'll stay and carry out the conditions of your contract.'

She glared belligerently. He looked like a man suffering agonies, and she despised him for being weak-willed, for allowing Alison to have her own way. 'What choice have I?'

'None!' He sounded sad. 'I'll keep you here by force if I have to.'

'I wish I'd never signed that damn piece of paper!' cried Susi crazily. 'I never thought it would come to this—I thought I'd enjoy working here. But if you think I shall enjoy seeing you with Alison you're mistaken. If that woman comes near me I shall scratch her eyes out, make no mistake about that!'

He smiled grimly, seeming to find pleasure in her harshly spoken words. 'I'll make sure she never comes to the house.'

That meant he would go to her! Susi wondered how she would get through the long hours when he was absent. Her vivid imagination already pictured the two of them together making love, making up for all the time they had lost. It was a heartbreaking thought, but there was nothing she could do about it, so she nodded and said, 'I promise, Latham. Can I go now?' There was a dull flatness to her tone, a finality in her voice. Her shoulders were bowed, her head drooped, and if she had looked up she would have seen the compassion in Latham's eyes. But she did not want to look at him again—ever. He had broken her heart, and although she supposed it would mend in time it would certainly not be during her enforced spell here.

'I'm sorry,' said Latham quietly as she walked brokenly along the corridor. 'I really am, Susi. Believe me, if I could have worked things out any other way I would have done.'

Susi had no idea what he was talking about. All she knew was that she had lost the only man she had ever loved to a woman who did not deserve him.

The next few days were sheer hell. She worked harder than ever—not because Latham forced her to but because it was the only way she could keep her mind occupied. He was away a lot of the time and she knew he was with Alison, although true to his word, he never brought her to the stud.

Susi had never known such anguish. The coming twelve months would be the longest year she had ever spent. Already she had toyed with the idea of using her wages to get away, but always something stopped her.

And not the fact that Latham held her to her contract. She didn't care a fig about that. It was the man himself. Despite the fact that he had swung his attentions back to Alison, Susi could not bring herself to leave. It was self-inflicted torture, but she felt she deserved the punishment for being so stupid as to allow herself to become involved in the first place.

Not that they had had an affair, but it had bordered on one, and she had been quite sure that before long they would have both become intensely emotionally involved.

Jake grumbled incessantly about the way she was driving herself. 'You'll make yourself ill. Why are you doing it? Anyone would think Latham held a whip over you!'

Susi looked at him tiredly. 'Has he told you he's back with Alison?'

The old man shook his head. 'He doesn't say much, but I've seen for myself what's going on. He needs his head examining, if you ask me. Is that why you're working so hard, trying to get him out of your system?'

Susi nodded wryly. 'Things were beginning to look good when she appeared on the scene. I hate her!'

'I've no doubt the feeling is mutual,' gruffed Jake sagely. 'But I shouldn't worry about her. Latham's too intelligent to let a woman of her kind run rings round him.'

'When you're in love it's amazing what you do,' said Susi, knowing how stupidly she was behaving herself. 'It warps your judgment, and Latham's got it good and proper where Alison's concerned. I don't think he ever stopped loving her. I expect any day now he'll announce their engagement.' And when that day came she would go.

She would not hang around once he was totally committed to Alison. Until then there was always the slim chance that their relationship would fail once again.

Jake continued to shake his head, his pale watery eyes troubled. 'He needs someone to give him a talking to, but the trouble is he won't listen. I tried to tell him once what that girl was like, long before she ran out on him, but he would have none of it. He listens only to the voices of his heart.

'I didn't fall in love with my wife until after we were married. We had a good relationship, we were friends, we shared the same interests, and were very fond of each other, but it was not until after we'd lived together, discovered each other's faults, that I could actually say I fell in love with her. It developed over the years and was more deep and lasting than any of them so-called love at first sight marriages.'

This was a long speech for Jake to make, and Susi knew it made sense. He was perhaps trying to tell her that she was being stupid feeling about Latham the way she did. But although Jake hadn't loved his wife right from the beginning it did not mean that she could not be in love with Latham. She did love him. She wanted nothing more than to spend the rest of her life with him. She was quite sure that her love would never fade.

She smiled weakly. 'Thanks for telling me, Jake. I only wish it helped.'

'Just take it easy, Susi. You won't get thought any more of if you make yourself ill. One of the new hands Jake's taken on has taken quite a shine to you. He's single and not a bad-looking lad. Why don't you go out with him? You deserve some enjoyment.'

Susi looked at Jake sadly. 'How can you suggest such a thing? You know how I feel about Latham. I don't want to go out with anyone else.'

'It would do you good,' he insisted. 'I'll have a word with him, shall I?'

'You'll do no such thing!' declared Susi loudly. 'Besides, it wouldn't be fair. I'm not fit company for any man at the moment.'

But during lunch she caught the eye of Chuck Allen on her and was not altogether surprised when he stayed behind. He was a fresh-looking young man with a round cheerful face and an engaging grin. 'How'd you like to come into Sydney with me tonight?' he asked. 'I got paid today, so we can paint the town red. You sure don't seem to have much excitement around here.'

Susi eyed him coldly. 'I told Jake I didn't want to go out with you. Hasn't he relayed the message?'

'Oh, yes,' admitted Chuck candidly, 'but women usually change their minds. It's their prerogative. So how about it? You need some enjoyment. You work too hard.'

'Perhaps I like it. Don't you think that could be the reason?'

He shrugged. 'So do I, but I like to have fun as well. Come on, what harm is there in it? I bet I can show you a side of Sydney that you've not yet seen.'

I bet you can, thought Susi, envisaging the sort of places that he would enjoy, but still with no intention of going anywhere with him.

Unperturbed by her attitude, Chuck continued, 'We'll leave about seven. Be ready,' and disappeared out of the kitchen before she could say another word.

Susi smiled ruefully. He did not seem a bad lad and she supposed there was no harm in one date. It would be infinitely better than sitting alone torturing herself with thoughts of Latham and Alison.

She prepared a salad for Jake—and Latham—although she doubted whether he would come home early. It was usually late when he got in, and she never fell asleep before he did. One night he had not come home at all, and she had lain awake the whole time wondering how much longer she could stand the suffering.

When Chuck Allen popped his cheerful head round the kitchen door at seven on the dot she was ready. Guessing what sort of places he was likely to take her to, she wore jeans and a cool top, her suspicions confirmed when she saw that he wore jeans too.

'I'm glad you changed your mind,' he grinned. 'Though I knew you would. Women always do.'

'Hark at you!' she quipped, smiling as she followed him out to his car. She quite liked this young man. He was different from Latham and would certainly help her forget her troubles for an hour or two.

His car rattled along as though ready to fall to pieces at any second. 'What do you think of my boneshaker?' he asked proudly.

Susi grinned. 'If it gets us from A to B that's all that matters.'

'Wish I could afford a Mercedes like the boss,' he grumbled goodnaturedly, 'or I wouldn't mind that little sports car. I could fancy myself in that. Been out with him, have you?'

'A couple of times,' admitted Susi.

'Been working here long?'

'Two months.'

'Two weeks, me, and I doubt I'll be here much longer. I like to travel about, get bored in one spot for too long. What brought you out here? Got relatives in Australia?'

It was a perfectly innocent question, but Susi could not help feeling disturbed. 'My brother,' she admitted reluctantly.

'So why aren't you living with him?'

'He's moved house,' explained Susi, 'and I haven't been able to trace him yet. I need money to do that, so I took this job.'

Chuck looked interested. 'What's his name? I meet a lot of people, I might know him.'

'Carl Kingswood,' supplied Susi eagerly, watching his face for a sign of recognition. But there was none.

'Sorry,' he said at last. 'But I'll keep my eyes and ears skinned. If I come across him I'll let him know where you are.'

'I'd prefer that you tell me where he is,' said Susi. 'I—
I'd like to surprise him.' She could not say that her own
brother had refused to see her. It would look very funny
indeed.

'You puzzle me,' he said. 'You're not the usual kind
of girl that I meet. You work so hard for one thing, and
you never go out.'

She shrugged. 'Like you say, there's nothing much to
do about this place, not without transport.'

He agreed. 'Tell you what, when I leave here you can
have mine. 'I've got plans—big plans—I shan't need
this old car.'

'I might just take you up on that,' laughed Susi. 'If
it's still in one piece. It will be nice to go out on my own
without having to wait for a lift from Latham.'

But somehow the idea of her own car was no longer
so important. The reason she had wanted a vehicle was
to find Carl—and there was only Alison who knew his
whereabouts. Now that Latham was back with the
sultry blonde she could not very well go to see her.

'How friendly are you with him?' he asked. 'Seems to
be out a lot. I've hardly seen him since I've been here. A
girl, is it?'

Susi shrugged. 'He doesn't discuss his affairs with
me.' And there was something in the way she spoke that
told Chuck she had no wish to discuss their mutual
employer.

He flashed her a wry grin. 'Okay, subject closed.
Who shall we talk about—you? You're the prettiest-
looking girl I've seen in a long time. How come you're
not married?'

'Maybe because no one's asked me,' she tossed
smartly, smiling all the same. Chuck Allen was easy to
get on with.

'Then maybe I stand a chance?'

'Afraid not,' said Susi. 'Let's get this straight from the start: I'm not interested in men.'

'Funny woman,' he shrugged. 'But you can't blame a guy for trying. I'm sure not going to let it spoil my evening.' He put his foot down even harder on the accelerator. The car jolted and jerked along and Susi was too busy holding on to the edge of her seat to indulge in further conversation.

But all the time she was with Chuck Susi's thoughts were with Latham. She could not get him out of her mind. Although Chuck was fun and she would have liked to give him her undivided attention her mind kept wandering. She wondered if Latham was dining out with Alison, or whether they were alone in her flat making love. Each time it was like a knife turning in her heart.

They had eaten at a Chinese restaurant in the centre of Sydney and were now sitting in a disco where flashing lights and loud music made talking impossible.

When he had unsuccessfully tried to say something to her two or three times Chuck caught her hand and pulled her outside. 'I think that's enough of that,' he laughed, holding his ears comically. 'What I was trying to say was, whoever the guy is he's not worth it. Let your hair down and forget him. There's no point in being miserable.'

'How do you know it's a man?' asked Susi. She had not realised her unhappiness was so clear.

'When a woman looks like you do it's always a man. And if he hasn't the good sense to recognise a beautiful woman then he's not worth breaking your heart over. Come on, let's go and have a saunter down Kings Cross.'

Susi eyed him warily. She had heard about Kings Cross. It was Sydney's equivalent to Soho, or Paris's

Pigalle, full of strip joints, sex shops and sleazy nightclubs. She was not sure that she wanted to go there.

Chuck saw the hesitation on her face. 'It's a must,' he said. 'You can't come to Sydney and not see the Cross. It's like going to London and not looking at Buckingham Palace.'

His unlikely comparison amused her and she laughed, allowing herself to be led in the direction of this infamous area, holding on to Chuck's arm as they got nearer.

'Many years ago it was the centre of Sydney's bohemian life,' he told her grandly. 'Unlike today when it has two faces. By day it is, believe it or not, a staid residential and shopping area.'

'And by night,' smiled Susi, 'there's a dramatic change. I think I'd rather come in the daytime.' She shivered and clung more tightly.

Neon lights lit up the branches of the trees. It was a weird electric place and Susi tried not to look at the prostitutes who fluttered their over-long lashes at any likely-looking male who passed.

There were groups of tourists like herself armed with cameras, speculating whether a leather-clad youth sitting beneath the fountain was a drug pusher, staring curiously at the girls in their alluring dresses. It was not the sort of place that Susi would have cared to walk through alone, not at night anyway, but it was an experience. There were groups of youths on motorcycles, others crowded on street corners, all finding pleasure in this dubious place.

Chuck took her inside one of the nightclubs that looked less garish than any of the others and they sat and drank until Susi declared it was time they went home.

It was not until they were in Chuck's car that she realised how late it was, and they were made even later when he had a puncture on the way. Although it had nothing to do with Latham what she did in her spare time she hoped they would be home before him, knowing that he would be displeased if he discovered she had been out with Chuck Allen.

Not that there was anything he could do about it. Chuck wasn't married like the rest of them and if she wanted to go out with him then that was her business. Except that she had not enjoyed the evening very much. It was Latham she would much rather be out with.

When they arrived at Kalabara Susi was relieved to observe that Latham's car was still missing. She thanked Chuck for taking her out. 'Don't mention it,' he said. 'We must do it again.' He made no attempt to kiss her and she was glad.

She had been in her room no more than a few minutes when she heard Latham's car pull up outside. Normally he went straight to bed, but tonight he surprised her by pounding on her door and bursting in without waiting for an answer.

'Where the hell have you been?' His face was tight with anger, his arms hanging loosely at his sides, fingers curled as though he was having difficulty in keeping them off her.

'Out,' she said quietly. 'And it's no business of yours.'

'I like to know where you are.'

'You're my employer, not my keeper,' she returned sharply. 'If I want to go out then I will. As a matter of fact I've had a very pleasant evening with Chuck Allen.'

'So I understand,' he growled. 'Jake told me. I came back early. I was going to take you out myself. You had no right going without telling me.'

'No right?' yelled Susi, even as she groaned inwardly. What a golden opportunity she had lost! But she was not going to admit that it bothered her. 'I can do what the hell I like. But why did you want to take me out? Has Alison thrown you over yet again?'

'Let's leave Alison out of this,' he growled. 'I want to know what you've been doing—all of it. Has that guy made love to you?'

Susi could not believe that she was hearing him correctly. 'Really, Latham, do you think I'd tell you if he had? What I do in my own time is my affair and has nothing at all to do with you.'

'If he's laid one finger on you,' he grated, 'I swear I'll break every bone in his body.'

Susi's heart jolted painfully. He sounded as though he was jealous—which was ridiculous when she meant nothing to him. But it excited her seeing him like this and some devil drove her on. 'At least I know where I stand with Chuck. There are no pretences between us.'

'Are you going out with him again?'

'He's asked me to,' admitted Susi.

'I forbid it.' His voice vibrated round the room. He came over to her, his fingers biting into the soft flesh of her upper arms. 'I forbid it, Susi. Do you hear? That man's not worthy of you. He came here asking for a job and I gave him one. He'll be gone in a couple of weeks. He's an opportunist—we call them drifters. They have no particular skills and go from place to place getting work where they can. He's not your type at all, Susi.' He punctuated each word with a shake until Susi began to feel punch-drunk.

'I didn't say I was looking for a long-lasting relationship. Chuck's good fun, I enjoy being with him.'

'And you like him kissing you?' His lips thinned cruelly.

'Is it any business of yours?' asked Susi coldly. 'Please let me go—I'm tired. I want to go to bed.'

'It's a wonder you didn't invite your new friend into bed,' he snarled. 'But lucky for him you didn't, because if I'd found you together I'd——'

His grip tightened and she thought he was going to snap her bones, then he pulled her brutally against him, clamping his mouth on hers, bruising her lips, taking his anger out on her. Susi was too emotionally hyped up to stop him. For the last week she had thought of nothing except Latham kissing her, and even though he was now taking her in anger it was better than nothing.

She returned his kisses readily, arching her body against the rock-hard strength of him, feeling an aching awareness in the pit of her stomach. For the moment Alison was forgotten. Chuck Allen was forgotten. Latham was kissing her, and even though it meant nothing to him it meant everything to her.

As abruptly as he had taken her he pushed her roughly from him, sending her staggering across the bed. She looked up indignantly, trying to show an anger she was far from feeling. 'Why did you do that?' she demanded.

'Why?' His breathing was as ragged as hers, his eyes glazed. 'You tell me why you went out with Chuck Allen.'

'Because I'm fed up with staying in,' she blazed. 'Isn't that good enough?'

He inclined his head. 'Point taken, but did it have to be him?'

'Who else is there,' she demanded. 'Jake?'

He was not amused. 'Promise me you won't go out with Allen again?' There was an urgency in him that she could not understand.

'I don't see why I should, but I will if you'll promise

me one thing too.' She held her breath as she steadied herself for her request. 'Not to go out with Alison either.'

She was almost afraid to look at him, but she did, and saw the glimmer of pain cross his eyes. 'I'm sorry, that's impossible.' His voice was low and strained.

'Then don't try and stop me seeing my friends,' she cried angrily. 'And get out, *now!*' Taking off her shoe, she flung it at him.

Latham caught it and held it between his hands, looking down at it as if wondering why that missile had been intended for him. There was an aggrieved air about him as though he could not understand why she was acting in such a manner.

'I said get out!' she screamed.

He looked at her reproachfully, then putting the shoe down on the floor he opened the door and went out without saying another word.

Susi did not know for how long she sat on the bed. It was probably hours. In any case it was a long time before she found the strength to get undressed. Normally she took a shower before going to bed, but tonight she had neither the energy nor the inclination. She was upset because she had missed the opportunity of a night out with Latham, and even more disturbed by his unreasonable attitude.

Chuck issued another invitation the next day, but Susi refused. 'I'm tired,' she said quietly. It was a feeble excuse, but the only one she could think of.

'Some other time, then,' he said cheerfully, unperturbed by her rejection.

'Yes, some other time,' agreed Susi.

The next few days and nights Susi suffered agonies, convinced that Latham knew her every move, even though he was not at the stud himself. She had an idea

BRANDED   165

that he had asked Jake to watch her, for the old man
frequently seemed to be on the scene.

'I heard,' said Jake, 'that the boss laid into you for
going out with Chuck. I'm sorry about that. It was my
fault.'

'It wasn't, not at all,' said Susi, 'but don't worry, I
shan't go out with him again.' And Jake did not ask her
why. He knew how she felt about Latham.

But then one day when she was feeling particularly
low, when she was fed up with her own company night
after night, she accepted one of Chuck's repeated
invitations.

He took her to one of the floating restaurants on
Sydney harbour, and although she knew she should
not have let him she allowed him to kiss her when
they got home. But she felt no response at all and
when he pulled away with an apologetic air, she said,
'I'm sorry.'

He shrugged. 'Forget it, it's what I expected, but
for pity's sake don't go on eating your heart out for
some guy who's not interested. It won't do you any
good.'

She smiled weakly and made her way along the
corridor to her room. She was surprised to see a strip of
light beneath the door. Latham, she thought, her heart
plummeting. He had caught her again!

But she was her own mistress and there was nothing
he could do about it. He was the one who had chosen
to finish their affair almost before it started. He could
not dictate to her what she could or could not do. He
had no right. No right at all.

She bounced the last few steps and banged open the
door, her face full of anger, her eyes flashing savagely—
and then stopped dead in her tracks.

It had been a long time since she had seen the man

who was standing just a few feet away. He had
changed. But there was no mistaking that rich auburn
hair—the exact shade as her own—those grey-green
eyes.

'Carl!' she cried. 'Oh, Carl! Is it really you?'

CHAPTER EIGHT

To be held in the arms of her brother was something that Susi had not expected—not today at any rate—not for some time. The frustrations of the last few weeks dissolved in a flood of tears, and it was several minutes before she was able to speak. Carl held her as though she were still his baby sister, a child to be loved and consoled.

When at length she looked at him, lifting her face to gaze into his eyes, noting how much older he seemed than the boy who had left England eight years ago, she was overwhelmed with emotion. This man was all the family she had, he meant more to her than anyone else in the world.

More than Latham? asked a tiny voice inside her. And at this moment, yes, even more than Latham. Because loving Latham was pointless. One day she would finish here and walk out of his life and that would be the last she would see of him. But Carl, Carl would always be there.

'I'd begun to despair of ever seeing you,' she husked at length, her voice shaky with tears. 'Why did you refuse to see me?'

'There's so much to explain,' he said gruffly. 'The important thing is that I'm here now, but I never imagined, little Susi, that you'd come chasing after me like this. When I first heard you were in Australia I couldn't believe it. I remember you as a little girl with spindly legs and freckles. You sure turned into a beautiful woman! I never thought my kid sister would

develop like this.' He grinned, holding her at arm's
length, searching her face. 'If you weren't family I
reckon I'd fancy you myself!'

Susi smiled wryly. 'You'll never know how much
your coming here means to me.'

He looked contrite all of a sudden, then he let her go,
moving a few steps away before turning to look at her
again. His face was troubled. 'I'm not here voluntarily,
Susi. I've done a lot of things about which I'm
ashamed. I didn't want to see you. I felt I had no right
to involve you with my dishonour.'

'I'm family,' cried Susi. 'I'm automatically involved.
My God, Carl, don't ever think that! I want to help you
in any way I can. I'm a woman now, I'm not stupid or
silly like I was when you left home. I'll always stand by
you, Carl, you should know that.'

He kept shaking his head and she was not sure
whether it was because he was fighting an inner battle
to shut her out of his life, or whether it was because he
was still having difficulty in accepting how grown-up
she was.

'Are you on holiday?' he asked abruptly. 'Or are you
here to pave the way for Mum and Dad? I know they
always talked about settling here once Dad retired. He
must be about due.' And then, 'My God, I was so
excited seeing you I've forgotten to ask how they are!'

Susi closed her eyes, that aching grief crushing her
heart. She would never be able to think of her parents
without remembering the way they had died. 'Mum and
Dad are dead,' she burst out desperately, unable to coat
the bad news with honeyed words. 'It was—a—car
accident.'

Carl's face drained of colour. 'Oh, no! Oh, no! I kept
meaning to write. But I was so ashamed of myself. I
was waiting until——'

'They didn't suffer,' cut in Susi, hating to see the anguish on his face. 'They died instantly. It was a head-on collision with a lorry that had gone out of control. There was nothing at all Dad could have done.'

Her brother crumpled, sagging down on to the edge of the bed and burying his head in his hands. Susi stood silently and watched, knowing that he needed a few minutes to pull himself together. It had been a tremendous shock. She ought not to have blurted it out so cruelly. She ought to have prepared him.

At length Carl looked at her, and Susi's heart went out to him when she saw the sadness in his eyes, his tear-stained face. 'I'm sorry, I shouldn't have told you like that, but I've waited so long. It was the reason I came over here. I wanted to tell you personally, not put it in a letter. There's only me and you now, Carl.'

She sat beside him and he held her close. He was shaking and she knew that the shock was probably worse for him than it had been for her. He must be feeling as if the bottom had dropped out of his world. Even though he had not written she did not doubt that his love for his parents had never faded.

'There's so much to be said, little Susi. But this is such a shock—it's—I—I never expected it. Were they very hurt when I stopped writing?'

She nodded, unable to speak. She hated seeing Carl upset. He had always been her tough elder brother, a bit of a bully, and what she heard from Latham had merely confirmed that opinion. She hadn't known he had a heart.

With a superhuman effort he pulled himself together. 'I can't believe you're working for Latham. It's the last place I'd expect you to be.'

'I came here looking for you,' she said quietly. 'It was the only lead I had when you weren't at your Sydney flat.'

'And Latham didn't chuck you out?'

She smiled wryly. 'We had quite a set-to, I must admit.'

'And then he offered you a job? How did you manage that?'

'It was no offer,' she said strongly. 'He more or less forced me. He said that I'd do instead of you, that he would keep me here until he considered I'd paid your debts.'

'He what?' Carl clenched his fists and threw himself to his feet. The temper that she knew he possessed began to rise rapidly to the surface, flushing his face an ugly red.

'Please!' She caught his hand and pulled him down again. 'I didn't mind, I enjoyed it. He thought he was using me to score off you, but it backfired, because I liked what I was doing. Besides, I wanted to stay around until I found you. I'd got no money, I couldn't go back to England. In any case, there seemed no point. You've no idea how much it bothered me not to have any family. I was desperate to find you.'

'He didn't hurt you?' Carl took several deep breaths in an effort to regain control.

'No!' Susi shook her head firmly. 'He never did that.'

There must have been something in her voice that gave her away, because Carl said thickly, 'He didn't try anything else?'

It was not difficult to guess what he had in mind. Again Susi shook her head, but knew she looked guilty.

'Don't say you've fallen for him?' Carl looked horrified. 'Not Latham Elliot? I know he's a handsome beggar, or he was before I——' He stopped and looked uncomfortable all of a sudden.

Susi felt swift compassion, but guessed he did not need it at that moment. 'I'm afraid I have. He's some man, Carl, despite what you say. It's one-sided, though. Latham's back with Alison.'

'So I gather,' he said drily, 'but she's a bitch and no mistake. Much as I dislike the man, he deserves a better deal than her.'

Susi looked at her brother questioningly. 'I thought you and she were——?' She paused awkwardly.

'She helped me when I needed someone,' he admitted, 'and we once had an affair—but she'd give herself to any man with money. After the way she treated Latham, though, I'm sure as hell surprised he's had her back. How did you know that Alison and I were friends? Did Latham tell you?'

'You're joking,' she exclaimed quickly. 'It was Jake. He's sort of taken me under his wing and he wanted to help.'

'Or help Latham,' said Carl bitterly, 'to find me through you. You've no idea what a spot you put me in. It wasn't true that I didn't want to see you, but I had no choice. You see, I couldn't be sure that you wouldn't tell Latham—or that he'd drag it out of you. It's been murder these last two years. I knew that if Latham ever got his hands on me he'd kill me—and I didn't mean to hurt him. You must believe that, Susi. I was scared, scared because he'd caught me out, and I acted without thinking. There's not a day gone by since that I haven't regretted what happened.'

'Does Latham know you're here now?'

He nodded. 'But I'm not sure how long he'll be able to keep his hands off me. He said I could talk to you, but I don't trust that guy.'

'You have reason to be scared,' said Susi quickly. 'He hates your guts. But maybe if you explained that you've seen the error of your ways he'll——'

'He'll what?' interjected Carl savagely. 'Latham Elliot

hasn't a forgiving nature. Or don't you know him that well?'

She shook her head sadly. 'You're right, of course. He's after your blood, I've known that all along. You took a chance coming here, and I'm grateful, I really am. Tell me what you've been doing these last two years.'

He looked embarrassed. 'Getting help. I had a drink problem, you see. It was the root of all my troubles.'

'I can't see how drinking would have caused you to steal,' said Susi. 'Latham told me that you'd fiddled his books, that you owed him a considerable amount of money.'

Carl sighed. 'I'm not a very good brother, am I? I don't know why you want me. I suppose you may as well know now, I was in trouble in England. I did some shoplifting as a kid. Nothing much, and it wasn't as though I needed it, it was just the thrill of getting away with it. I thought when I moved to Australia I'd start a new life, but I'm afraid there were times when I was desperately short of money. And it was so easy, like taking candy from a baby.

'Of course, with money in my pockets I began to drink and date expensive women—Alison Cordell included. In the end I couldn't do without a drink, so I had to find ways of getting even more money. Looking back I can see how incredibly foolish I was. I've had treatment, Susi. I'm a reformed character now.'

'Does Latham know that?' She had listened carefully as Carl related his tale, feeling horror, then pity, now relief.

He shook his head, his face looking old and tired all of a sudden. 'We haven't said more than a couple of words to each other. I reckon once he's given me time to talk to you it'll all be over.'

'You could let me talk to him,' she said immediately. 'I'd explain, like you've explained to me. It will be all right, I know it will.'

'No,' Carl said thickly. 'You don't know Latham like I do. Once he's got something into his head nothing will get rid of it. He's gunning for me, and don't I know it!'

'Then we'll leave,' she said impulsively. 'We'll leave together. We'll go now, before he has time to find out what we're doing.'

He looked sceptical. 'In what? Have you got a car?'

Susi shook her head.

'Then how, tell me that?'

'How did you get here?' she frowned.

'Latham brought me.'

'Latham?' she echoed incredulously. This was the last thing she had expected to hear. But there was no time to ask how it had come about.

He nodded, lips compressed. 'I'm at his mercy, Susi. There's no escape now.'

'Nonsense!' she said strongly. 'I'm not going to let him kill you. We'll get away somehow. I have a friend, who has a car, and he said he'd give it to me when he left. He'll help, I know.' As she spoke she flung clothes into her suitcases, cramming them in anyhow and snapping the locks.

Carl picked them up. 'I sure hope you're right, Susi.'

She opened the door, checking that the corridor was empty. They saw no one as they made their way through the kitchen to the yard. Susi knew Chuck slept on a mattress in the barn, refusing Jake's offer to share his flat, and she had expected him to go straight there after their evening out. But it was empty, and when she looked in the corner of the yard where he kept his car that was missing too. She turned to Carl with despair on her face. 'He's gone! What are we going to do?' Her voice was agonised.

Before Carl had time to reply a figure emerged from the shadows. Susi froze and clutched her brother's arm anxiously.

'Going somewhere?' Latham's deep-throated voice sliced through the blackness.

For several heart-stopping seconds Susi could not speak. Carl stood tense at her side and they both looked at the arrogant man confronting them.

'Where's Chuck?' countered Susi aggressively, when she finally managed to find her tongue.

'Gone!' Latham's voice was dangerously soft.

'Your doing, I suppose?'

'It was necessary,' he said coldly, his mouth a thin hard line. 'I warned you about going out with him again.'

Susi's eyes narrowed. 'My private life has nothing to do with you.'

'Maybe, maybe not, but I have a right to hire and fire whom I please. Chuck was passing through. He's now moved on. Were you thinking of asking him to help?'

'You know very well I was!' Susi could not contain her hostility. She was angry because her plans had been thwarted and did not know what to do. It was difficult to believe that this was the man she loved. He had never been more distant from her, and right at this moment she hated him. Carl was of prime importance. She wanted to get him away.

Her brother had remained silent, now he said quietly to Susi, 'There's nothing more you can do. This is it.' He looked at his ex-employer, but before he could speak Susi said quickly, 'Carl's a reformed character, Latham. Did he tell you that? He's truly sorry for what he did.'

She eyed the scar and wondered whether Carl being sorry would really help when he had this perpetual reminder. 'He's been having treatment and no longer has a drinking problem. And now I'm here to help him I'm quite sure he'll never get into trouble again. Please, let us go.'

'It's right what Susi says,' admitted Carl. 'I am sorry, Latham, I never meant to hurt you. I lost my head. I'm doing pretty well now. I have my own truck and very soon I'll be able to pay you back the money I stole.'

Latham did not speak. He looked down at the two of them, his black brows knitted. There was no sign of forgiveness on his face, no indication that what they had said made any difference. 'I'd like a word with you, Carl,' he said at last. 'Alone.'

Susi clutched at her brother, but Carl released her fingers. 'Don't worry, Susi. It'll be all right.'

But Susi was not so sure. She still felt that Latham might hurt Carl. He had not said he believed him. She was afraid to leave the two of them together.

'Five minutes,' said Latham, 'that's all I need.'

Susi's head jerked, her eyes cold and accusing. 'Five minutes is long enough to kill a man.'

Even in the darkness she could see that her words had added to Latham's anger. His nostrils flared and his mouth became grim. She could actually see him striving to control himself. His fingers curled and uncurled at his sides, his magnificent chest heaved.

'I asked you to trust me, Susi. I'm not going to harm your brother, I give you my word. If that's not good enough then there's nothing I can do about it. I intend talking to Carl no matter what you say.'

He swung away and Carl gave Susi an apologetic smile before following.

He's going to his death cell, she thought dramatically, panicking, knowing she was blowing the whole thing up out of all proportion. But she was so afraid for Carl. She knew how strong Latham's feelings were—and with good reason. He would not accept that Carl had changed. He would need proof before he believed either of them.

She trailed after them slowly, pacing the corridor outside the office, checking her watch frequently. She could hear nothing. Five minutes passed, and then ten. She hurled herself at the door, banging it open, checking herself only when she saw the two men sitting calmly one on each side of the desk.

There was a bottle of whisky between them, but only Latham was drinking. It took no more than a fleeting second for Susi to privately congratulate Carl on not capitulating. Latham had probably tested him.

Her aggression drained when she saw no sign of anger on either of their faces, and she smiled weakly, shamefacedly. 'I thought—you were—so long—I wondered what was happening.'

'You mean,' Latham accused, 'you wondered whether I'd kept my word.' He spread his hands expressively. 'You see? No harm done. Your brother is all in one piece.'

Carl pushed himself to his feet, smiling tenderly down at his sister. 'We were just finished, and I'm tired. Latham's kindly offered me a bed for the night, so I'm going to turn in.'

'But I want to hear all about it,' protested Susi.

Carl shook his head. 'We'll talk in the morning. You look tired too. Why don't you go to bed?'

'I'd like a word with Susi myself,' said Latham.

She looked at him crossly. 'There's nothing I want to say to you.'

'Not even a thank-you for keeping my hands off your brother?'

'I still don't trust you,' she said. 'Your hatred's festered for two whole years. Don't tell me you can forget it just like that. You'll probably murder him while he lies in his bed. It's the only reason I can think why you've invited him to spend the night.'

His jaw muscles tightened, his eyes grew cold. He dismissed Carl with the flick of an imperious finger, and when the door was safely closed behind him turned on Susi savagely.

'I don't take kindly to comments like that!'

She tilted her head, green eyes flashing. 'Are you suggesting that I apologise?'

'I'm suggesting you take back your words.'

'No! I don't trust you, Latham, and that's the truth, whether you like it or not.'

'You don't think I'd have gone to the trouble of bringing Carl here, letting him talk to you, if I'd meant him any harm?'

'You swore you'd kill my brother if you ever caught up with him.'

'And I meant it—once.'

Susi looked at him sceptically. 'You mean you've—*forgiven* him?'

'Hardly that,' crashed Latham, 'but neither do I fancy a jail sentence myself. He's told me about the help and treatment he's been getting. He's even given me the name of his psychiatrist in case I want to check up. He claims he was sick when he attacked me, otherwise he would never have done it.'

'And you believe him?' Susi waited with bated breath for his reply.

'I'm reserving judgment. Only time will tell.'

'But you're giving him a chance?'

He nodded, a hard smile curving his lips.

And this time Susi knew he spoke the truth. 'Thank you,' she said simply. 'Thank you, Latham, I appreciate that more than you'll ever know.' She wanted to rush over and throw herself into his arms, but the thought of Alison stopped her. Alison was the girl Latham loved, she must never forget that.

Instead she turned and headed for the door. When he spoke her name her hand was already on the handle, but there was something in the tone of his voice that caused her pulses to take a sudden upward swing. Slowly she pivoted, meeting the enigmatic expression in his sexy black eyes as he paced the room towards her.

Her heart pounded with each step that he took, and when finally he halted inches away from her it boomed like a drum in her ears. He lifted his hands and caught her upper arms, looking deep into her eyes, searching, probing.

She knew he was going to kiss her and closed her eyes, lifting her face towards him. She had no idea why this was happening, nor indeed did she care. It was too good an opportunity to miss.

The tension in his fingers increased until they were biting into her, hurting, bruising, and when the expected kiss did not materialise she dared to look at him, shocked by the agonised desire on his face.

The next second he had released her, pushing her roughly away. 'This is insanity! Go to bed, Susi. I have no right to do that to you.' His voice was hoarse, gruff, full of pain.

'Why?' she whispered huskily. 'Why, Latham? I want you to kiss me, you must know that. Is it—Alison?' A painful lump rose in her throat, threatening to choke her.

His back was towards her now, shoulders hunched, facing the window, staring out into the blackness of the night. Myriad stars twinkled, cicadas chirred, but he was blind. He was disturbed, and Susi guessed it was because he felt he had been momentarily disloyal to Alison.

'Yes.' The admission was dragged out painfully. 'For God's sake, Susi, *go!*'

There was something wrong somewhere, but she could not put her finger on it. She made a hesitant move towards him, jumping back when he swung round, his face distorted with a peculiar emotion that seemed to be raging right through him, his scar standing out more livid than she had ever seen it.

Without attempting to argue further she turned and left, going straight to her room. Latham's attitude puzzled her, scared her. He was like a man demented. Some devil was raging inside him—something to do with herself—and Alison!

Undeniably he was in the grips of this woman, otherwise he would never have gone back to her. But it would appear he was also attracted to herself! Every bone in her body ached with longing. Too late she wished she had stood her ground. Maybe, if she played her cards right, she would stand a chance of winning him from Alison?

But would she be happy? Wouldn't she always wonder whether this other woman might beckon her finger one day—and he would go running, just as he had now? He must love her very much to forgive her. It made her chances of success very slight.

It would be best if she never saw Latham Elliot again. He was not good for her. He was the only man in the world who had ever made her feel unsure of herself. Always she had been in command of her emotions. Now she felt helpless, caught in a web of desire. Her sanity was threatened if she remained here any longer.

Besides, there was Carl to think of. Latham had not harmed him, but she felt that it was an uneasy truce. It would be much better if he left in the morning—and she went with him.

Many hours passed before Susi slept. In fact she seemed not to sleep at all. Long before dawn she heard Latham go out, driving his open-topped sports car like a madman. It was not difficult to guess where he was going.

She heard the harsh chuckle of a kookaburra, followed by the full orchestra in the treetops. Had birdsong ever been so poignant? It was as though they were trying to tell her that here was another beautiful day to be lived to the full.

With a sigh of resignation she pushed back the single sheet that was all the covering she needed, standing uninterestedly beneath the shower, wondering why she had fallen in love with a man who was totally besotted with another woman, who had no more than a simple physical interest in herself.

She looked at her cases which still stood where Carl had planted them the night before, in no doubt that she would be doing the right thing. It was the only way out, there was no other choice. Staying would be purgatory.

Not surprisingly Carl made no appearance at breakfast. He would not be sure of his reception. It was doubtful the other men would be as forgiving as Latham appeared to be. She still had reservations about his acceptance of her brother. It was an extremely volatile situation.

As soon as the men had gone, though, Carl came into the kitchen. He grinned cheerfully as she set a plate of bacon and eggs in front of him, not seeming too perturbed by the fact that he was in the house of a man who had threatened to kill him. In fact he looked completely at ease.

Susi scowled blackly. 'What are you looking so happy about?

'It's a beautiful day,' he said. 'My beautiful sister, who I thought never to see again, is here. What more could a guy want?'

She frowned. 'I think we ought to go as soon as you've eaten. I don't trust Latham. We'll ring for a taxi and get away before he comes back.'

'No need,' smiled Carl reassuringly. 'Latham said that unless there's a real urgency for me to go I can stay on a few days.'

'Why?' Susi was immediately suspicious. Latham had no reason to be so accommodating. In fact he had every excuse to boot Carl out now that contact had been made between the two of them.

Carl shrugged. 'All I can say is that he's a more than generous man.'

'Too generous,' snapped Susi. 'He must have a motive. It's best we leave. I was only staying until I'd found you. Now I have no reason at all to remain.'

'Not even the fact that you love Latham?'

She grimaced. 'That's the main reason why I must go. You've no idea what it's like loving a person who loves someone else. It's painful in the extreme. Please, Carl, let me come and live with you.'

He shook his head sadly. 'Even if I wanted to, Susi, it wouldn't work. I live in a tiny bedsitter and share a kitchen. There's no room for anyone else.'

'We could find a bigger place,' she insisted.

'It's not that easy. I took it because it's cheap. It suits me. I'm sorry, Susi, but that's the way it is. You're far better to go on working for Latham, getting a decent wage. If you upped and left you might not get another job. It's not worth being short of money. Don't forget I know what it's like. I've gone through a bad patch, and I have no wish to get into trouble again.'

Susi thought he was being unnecessarily cruel.

'There's no reason why I shouldn't get a job,' she argued. 'I'm pretty well qualified.'

'Ah, yes,' he smiled wickedly, 'I remember Mum writing to say you were at college. Pretty odd choice of career for a girl. How did you do?'

'Admirably,' she said smartly. 'And I had a jolly good job before I left England. I have excellent references, so I can't see any problems about finding employment. You don't want me with you, is that it?'

He sighed impatiently. 'Don't make this harder for me, Susi, than it already is. I'm telling you the truth. For the first time in my life I'm going straight. I intend to make it a success. And moving somewhere bigger, which will probably cost more than I can afford at the moment, is no answer.'

Susi saw no point in arguing any longer. She looked at him sullenly. 'How did Latham find you?' It was something that had puzzled her right from the moment Carl admitted that Latham had brought him here.

'Alison!' he said abruptly.

It came as no surprise. The woman would think she was doing Latham a good turn.

'I must admit I was pretty scared when he came,' continued Carl. 'As soon as I heard the pounding on my door I knew it was him. I'd been expecting him for so long, and when I heard you were in Australia I knew it was inevitable.'

'But I wouldn't have told him,' protested Susi.

He shook his head. 'He'd lain quiet. He could have found me if he'd really wanted to. I guessed you'd stir things up.'

'What I can't understand,' said Susi, 'is why he didn't go for you. He'd threatened it often enough.'

Carl shrugged. 'He wasn't exactly friendly. But he seemed more concerned about you. He said I was giving you a raw deal, that at least I should have the decency to talk to you.'

Susi's eyes shot wide. 'You're kidding! Why should he bother about me?'

'Perhaps,' said Carl slowly, 'he cares about you?'

'Rubbish!' snapped Susi, although it was a heady thought all the same. 'I once felt we might have something going for us. Everything pointed that way. Then Alison appeared on the scene and I was out of the running. He's shown no interest in me at all since. In fact I rarely see him.'

'It wasn't the impression I got,' said Carl. 'Perhaps he's a bit afraid of showing his feelings? It was a fine mess I made of his face, I never realised. He probably feels it wouldn't be fair to saddle you with him.'

'It's never bothered me,' protested Susi angrily. 'That's why I can't understand why he's going back to Alison. My God, I reckon she did him more harm than you did! Plastic surgery could get rid of his scars, but there's no way you can repair mental damage. She destroyed him completely, Carl. I've never seen a man in such a state. He felt he had no right to even date another woman. He seemed to think he was some sort of monster.'

'Hell,' said Carl. 'It's not that bad.'

'Try telling Latham,' she returned. 'For two years he's not been out with a woman. It's not natural! A couple of times he let his façade slip, but that's all. I find him overpoweringly attractive, Carl. He's the sexiest man I've ever met. My bones turn to water if he so much as looks at me. You think I'm being silly? Well, maybe I am, but that's the way it is.'

'You've told him how you feel?' asked Carl tenderly.

'Heavens, no!' cried Susi. 'What would be the point in telling Latham I love him, when it's Alison he cares about?'

'I think he would find it extremely interesting.' Latham's deep-throated growl came from behind her.

Susi spun on her heel, colour flooding her cheeks. 'How long have you been there?' she demanded sharply, and to Carl through her teeth, 'Why the hell didn't you tell me?'

'Because,' said Latham quietly, 'your brother felt I had a right to know. I mean, a guy does like to hear these things, preferably from the girl in question herself.'

'You had no right listening!' Susi felt distinctly uncomfortable.

'In which case,' said Latham, 'I would never have found out. Your revelation was certainly enlightening.'

She could not look at him. Her admission had not been intended for his ears. He had no right eavesdropping.

'I think,' he continued slowly, 'that it's about time you and I had a talk. I'm going to drag you away from your brother. There are things I have to say that are for your ears alone.'

Susi felt breathless as he took her elbow and led her firmly from the kitchen to her own room. He had not been angry. In fact he had seemed interested, and pleased! Was it a fillip to his male ego that she had fallen for him despite his facial disfiguration? Added to the fact that Alison had also taken him back, that must make him feel very good indeed, a whole man again. But she could not see where her confession would get her. There was no place for her in his life.

No sooner were they in her room than he pulled her against his hard pulsating body, wrapping her tightly in his arms. 'There is one thing,' he said thickly, his mouth already claiming hers, 'that must be taken care of before anything else. I can wait no longer.'

It was a kiss like no other kiss, making Susi forget time and reason. It transported her to the heights and she stayed there, responding totally, giving herself without restraint.

Time later to wonder why. For the present she took all he had to offer—and goodness knows there was plenty of that! His hands feverishly explored her body, stroking, teasing, arousing in her a desire so deep and wanton that she wondered whether she would ever be able to banish him from her thoughts.

It was as though Latham had a deep insatiable thirst, drinking from her lips, draining her. Never had she been so erotically aroused. Entirely new sensations pulsed through each and every nerve, and when finally he put her from him she felt bereft.

'God, I needed that,' he said hoarsely. He looked as tense and disturbed by the depth of their feelings as she was herself. They had been like two animals with a rapacious hunger for the other. It was an experience that left Susi trembling, her limbs so weak that she was compelled to sink down on the bed.

Latham joined her, not letting her go as she relaxed, lying by her side, holding her possessively. 'Tell me to my face what I heard you telling your brother,' he said thickly. 'I want to know I didn't imagine it.'

'What's the point?' Her voice was sad, even though her eyes still shone from the effect of his kisses. 'I didn't ever want you to know. Now you do it's going to make it all the harder to bear.'

'You're insane,' he said gently, tracing the outline of her lips with his finger. 'I want to hear you say it. Now! This moment!' His eyes were narrowed, thick lashes hiding their black depths.

Susi wondered whether they were as alive as her own. Whether Latham had been to heaven and back and wanted to go there again. He was so good at hiding his feelings. But he could not stop the pulse beating nervously in his jaw, or the trembling of his fingers as they rested against her cheek. They told her more than any words that he had not been unmoved by her response.

But to admit to a love that was pointless? She swallowed painfully, her eyes not leaving his as the admission was dragged from her. 'I love you, Latham. There, are you satisfied now that you've humiliated me?' Tears pricked the back of her eyes and she closed her lids quickly before they could spill over and give her away.

'The fact that I'm—disfigured——' He touched his face, allowing his fingertips to trace the whole length of the cicatrice, 'makes no difference to you?'

She shook her head, looking at him again, seeing him through the mist of her tears. 'I don't even notice—and that's the truth, whether you believe it or not.'

'You sweet child, I do believe you.' Latham drew a deep rasping breath, folding her in his arms, crushing her against him until she thought her lungs were about to collapse. 'You're the one person who's never, ever, let it affect you. I used to think it did, but that was me being foolish. I realise now that the times you drew away were because you—felt something for me. You tried to tell me, but I wouldn't believe you. You didn't want me to touch you because I'd made it clear that I had no intention of ever committing myself to another woman. Is that right—or am I being conceited?'

'It's right,' admitted Susi shyly.

'God, what a fool I've been!' he groaned. 'I should have known Alison's reaction wasn't everyone else's. That day we picnicked on the beach, I had such high hopes, and then everything went so damnably wrong. I spent the next day trying to sort myself out. I should have listened to you. I should have believed that you above all people wouldn't lie, that when you said you didn't find me repulsive you meant it.

'You're quite sure? It will be too late once we're married, because I don't believe in divorce. I must admit I once thought I'd found the right person—until she showed her true colours. But I don't think I've made a mistake this time. I'm crazy about you, Susi. You've no idea how I've prayed for you to fall in love with me—but I never really thought it would happen.'

Susi listened in a daze. It all seemed too good to be true. 'Are you trying to tell me that you love me, too, Latham? Or is it simply that because I want to hear it I'm misconstruing everything you say?'

'I love you,' he said softly, 'with every breath in my poor branded body. I think I loved you from the first moment you walked into my life.'

'Is that why you kept me here?'

He nodded, smiling wryly. 'If I hadn't been immediately attracted I'd have kicked you out, make no mistake about that. And you've no idea how many times I've told myself you're no good for me. You reminded me too much of Carl—and God, how I hated him!'

'Do you still?' Susi put her question softly, hesitantly.

'Not hate,' he said after a moment's thought. 'In fact I think I feel sorry for him. He's been through a far greater torment than me. But it looks as if he's seen the light. And, because he's your brother, I'm prepared to—tolerate him. I can't say I'll ever actually love the guy, but at least I don't feel that griping hatred any longer.'

'I'm glad,' Susi said simply. 'But if you love me, Latham, why have you been seeing Alison? Are you being fair on her? Or on me, for that matter? You can't love two women at the same time.'

'You think I love her?' He sounded incredulous. 'That bitch? God, no—no way!'

'Then why did you go back to her? It crucified me when you did, considering what she'd done to you. I decided you must be so deeply in love that you were prepared to forgive her.'

'I'll never forgive her,' he said strongly. 'Not as long as I live. And I told her that in no uncertain terms this morning. She didn't take to it kindly, but she'll get over it. Before long she'll be convincing some other poor guy that he's the right one for her.'

Susi shook her head. 'But you still haven't told me why you've been seeing her.'

Latham looked pained. 'She had me over a barrel. She promised to give me Carl's address if I agreed to resume our—er—relationship.' Susi gasped but did not interrupt. 'She took her time about it, I'm afraid, and there was nothing I could do except play along with her little game until I'd got what I wanted.'

'I'm surprised you let him see me first.' A lump in Susi's throat threatened to choke her.

'Hell, I didn't do it simply to get my hands on him, as you must know. I did it for you. I couldn't bear to see you unhappy about Carl. Your loyalty to him was a credit to you. I found him for you, my love.'

'You mean you—never really wanted to see Alison, that you—forced yourself to—to continue your affair—for my sake?' Susi felt humble.

'That was her intention,' he admitted, 'but things never did get back on the same footing. You don't really think I could bring myself to make love to her after what she did to me?'

'I'd like to think not,' admitted Susi, 'but she is an

attractive woman—and obviously used to getting her own way.'

'Not from me,' he snarled, 'but enough about Alison. She no longer exists so far as I'm concerned—and you're not to think about her either. She's bad for both of us.'

Susi snuggled up against him, feeling a warm glow spread through her limbs until she was totally enveloped. 'I think, Mr Elliot,' she smiled, 'that I'm going to enjoy being Mrs Elliot. I might even let you persuade me to give up my career!'

'I'd never do that,' he said. 'I believe in a woman being allowed to do her own thing.' Susi raised a mocking eyebrow, but he ignored her. 'Though I can't say I'd be happy with you out at work every day.'

'Nor me,' said Susi. 'It suddenly means nothing to me. I'd much rather stay here and work for you.'

'Not *for* me, my love, *with* me,' Latham groaned. 'We'll be a team.'

She pressed her lips to his scar, feeling him grow tense, and then as suddenly relax. 'Just think,' she said, 'if Carl hadn't done this to you we might not have met. I'd have found him at his flat and never made my way out here.'

'You have a point,' he admitted, kissing her with renewed hunger. 'Perhaps he's not such a bad guy after all!'

Here is a selection of Mills & Boon novels to be published at about the same time as the book you are reading.

HOUSE OF DISCORD	*Jane Arbor*
GREEK ISLAND MAGIC	*Gloria Bevan*
A DEEPER DIMENSION	*Amanda Carpenter*
THE FACE OF THE STRANGER	*Angela Carson*
SERPENT IN PARADISE	*Rosemary Carter*
NEW NURSE AT ST BENEDICT'S	*Lilian Chisholm*
MARRIAGE UNDER FIRE	*Daphne Clair*
A RULING PASSION	*Daphne Clair*
HEART OF GOLD	*Kay Clifford*
GUARDIAN DEVIL	*Linda Comer*
A BAD ENEMY	*Sara Craven*
BURDEN OF RICHES	*Helen Dalzell*
TANGLE OF TORMENT	*Emma Darcy*
THE GATES OF RANGITATAU	*Robyn Donald*
A MISTAKE IN IDENTITY	*Sandra Field*
FALKONE'S PROMISE	*Rebecca Flanders*
A MODERN GIRL	*Rebecca Flanders*
THE PRICE OF FREEDOM	*Alison Fraser*
PROPHECY OF DESIRE	*Claire Harrison*
BEYOND RUBIES	*Rosalie Henaghan*
FOR EVER AND A DAY	*Rosalie Henaghan*
EVER AFTER	*Vanessa James*
GENTLE PERSUASION	*Claudia Jameson*
FORGOTTEN PASSION	*Penny Jordan*
MAN-HATER	*Penny Jordan*
SAVAGE ATONEMENT	*Penny Jordan*
PACIFIC APHRODITE	*Madeleine Ker*
VIRTUOUS LADY	*Madeleine Ker*
DANGEROUS ENCOUNTER	*Flora Kidd*
DARKNESS OF THE HEART	*Charlotte Lamb*
A SECRET INTIMACY	*Charlotte Lamb*
CARIBBEAN CONFUSION	*Mary Lyons*

£5.95 net each

Welcome
to the Wonderful World
of Mills & Boon Romance

Interesting, informative and entertaining, each Mills & Boon Romance is an appealing love story.

Mills & Boon Romances take you to faraway places — places with real people facing real love situations — and you may become part of their story.

As publishers of Mills & Boon Romances we're extremely proud of our books (we've been publishing them since 1909). We're proud also that Mills & Boon Romances are the world's most-read romances.

Fourteen new titles are published every month and if you would like to have details of all available Mills & Boon Romances please write to:

Mills & Boon Reader Service,
P.O. Box 236,
Thornton Road,
Croydon, Surrey CR9 3RU.

North American readers should write to:
Harlequin Reader Service,
M.P.O. Box 707,
Niagara Falls,
N.Y. 14302.

Canadian Address: Stratford, Ontario, Canada.

We sincerely hope you enjoyed reading this Mills & Boon Romance.

Yours truly,
THE PUBLISHERS
Mills & Boon Romances